MRITYUSUTRA

Mahadevan Thampi

Translated from the Malayalam by

Radhika P. Menon

Published by Legend Times Group
51 Gower Street, London, WC1E 6HJ
info@legendtimesgroup.co.uk | www.legendpress.co.uk

The right of the above author to be identified as the author of this work has
been asserted in accordance with the Copyright, Designs and Patents Act
1988. British Library Cataloguing in Publication Data available.

First Edition

Translated from the Malayalam by Radhika P. Menon

Paperback ISBN: 978-1-918291-94-0

S. MAHADEVAN THAMPI is a renowned media consultant, journalist, short story writer and novelist in Malayalam (an Indian language). He has more than 15 titles to his credit, including novels like *Alakalillaatha Kadal* (*Serene Ocean*), *Jalaparvam* (*The Saga of Water*), *Azadi* (*Freedom*), *Himameghangal* (*Snowy Clouds*) and anthologies of short stories like *Aparaahnangal* (*Afternoons*), *Aakaashangalude Avakaashikal* (*Inheritors of the Skies*) and so on. Many of his works have been translated into English, Tamil, Kannada, Hindi, Sanskrit and even Turkish. Mahadevan Thampi has won numerous awards for his literary contributions to Malayalam, including the Devaswom Board Award, the Madhava Mudra Puraskaram, the SICL Award by the government of Kerala, and the Uroob Award.

RADHIKA P. MENON has translated more than 15 works from Malayalam to English.

She won the ICWT (International Center for Writing and Translation Award) of the University of California, Irvine in 2011 for *Tales of Athiranippadam*, along with Sreedevi K. Nair.

Her translation of Priya Joseph's Malayalam short story *Maaniyum Indira Gandhiyum* was longlisted for the John Dryden Translation Award by the University of Leeds in 2024.

Her translation of K. K. Kochu's *Dalithan* won the KLF Book of the Year in the Non-fiction category in 2025.

Her translations, Nandini Menon's *Aamcho Bastar* and N. N. Pillai's autobiography, *Yours Truly*, are forthcoming.

"There are more things in heaven and earth, Horatio, than are dreamt of in your philosophy."

Hamlet, IV, i

Salutations, ancient earth! O Mother! May I take leave?
The key to the globe-room, I return.

Mahakavi P. Kunjiraman Nair

ONE

A red blob sprang out of the sun. It was fiery in the beginning. Many other blobs too had flung themselves out from the sun in a similar manner. They also had found the inner moral qualms insufferable. How could this self-immolation be endured? But the sun did not spare even a single one that had escaped far into the remote distance, sailing through the vast expanses of timeless, empty, interstellar space. All of them were shackled to certain rhythms.

Didn't you try to flee? You deserve commensurate punishment!

That was the solar ire speaking.

Acknowledge my blazing feet and circumambulate me – for all eternity! Let your bodies roll on your orbit-floors around me as a votive ritual in expiation.

O Sun! What a punishment! And how long back it had begun! Guru Arya looked at the earth.

Shuro baahushu lokoyam Lambate putra vatsadah.

The earth hangs, like a tiny son clinging to the hero's arm. Poor dear!

O Vasundhara! Bearer of wealth! What a state you are in! Is this your fate? In this numbness of frozen time, you wait for the leaves of the seasonal cycles to fall? Even while rotating on your axis and simultaneously revolving in this suspended state. Do you think that one day the sun will take pity and release you?

Akrodhena jayet krodham

Calm conquers anger.

Do you think you can beat anger by being free of anger? If so, O Vasundhara, O earth! You are mistaken. You will gain liberty only after all these solar flares have died down. And that is impossible in this *yuga*, this aeon. If you wish to escape, you must leave this orbit. But do you have the physical and the mental strength for it?

O Vasundhara, O earth! You found the severity of this self-punishment unbearable! Maybe that was why you cursed the human race, taking care to spare all other living creatures that took birth from your womb. You have made eternal sorrow and suffering inevitable in human life. And you have made humans your prisoners.

O Vasundhara! I see in you an urge to inflict torture on others. I know that when your fiery rage and disappointments reach a peak, it is your habit to gather your thick tresses and tie them up into a knot bun at the top of your head. Now I notice that you have piled up all the stray strands of wandering dark clouds, and carelessly wound them into an impossible knot, with the evil intent of denying humans even the remains of the seasonal cycles!

Maybe you feel repulsed and disgusted with them for their unending greed, their splitting of you – with your forests, hills, seas and lands, continents, islands and island clusters – into several nations, big and small, fixing boundary walls for their separate portions, and yet expanding their borders. That may be the reason for your anger towards humanity.

Maybe you have feelings of vengeance and bitterness towards those who have mauled and scooped out your soil-body; dug deep into your ocean-viscera; sucked out minerals and oil from your blood, bone and marrow; levelled your private parts of undulating hills and mountains; most cruelly set ablaze the fluffy, downy hair of your meadows; dried up the clear founts trickling from your kind, melting heart; and thus completely destroyed your equilibrium. That too may be the reason for your vengeful attitude towards humans.

Maybe you are provoked to anger on seeing humans not only rob and thieve their way into forests but also send fear-driven animals to seek food and water in human habitats, and then crack open their jaws using traps, leave them half-dead using live electric wires or splinter their heads using guns. Maybe you are moved to compassion on seeing the dead animals. That too may be the reason for your hatred towards humankind.

But O Vasudha, O holder of treasures! I have made a decision to liberate all human beings on this planet from all sorrow and troubles. I will implement my decision. I will rescue all humans. The time has come.

My journey has begun.

TWO

Guru Arya stood at the foot of the saffron hill like an outsider. His matted hair and long beard swayed in the breeze. His eyes sparkled with an otherworldly glow.

Very quickly, Guru Arya understood that somebody had labelled the earth with the symbolic term 'saffron hill'. The earth was a different saffron hill in each different place. So, there were many saffron hills. Yet, all had the same identity. The same rituals had been organised at every saffron hill for all time, and they went on relentlessly.

Guru Arya was convinced of the fact when he saw it directly.

It was Megharoopan who saw Guru Arya for the first time. He had been laboriously carrying a load of soil on his head to the crest of the saffron hill when he spotted a radiant-looking *sanyasi* standing there with his gaze fixed on the hill.

That face looks so divine! Those eyes have such a commanding power!

Megharoopan even felt that there was a supernatural aura enveloping the sanyasi.

As he stood there, gaping with wonderment and respect, his headload shifted, upsetting his poise. Megharoopan swayed a bit, and before he knew it, one of the rocks he had climbed over, slid and tumbled down. It rolled and almost reached the feet of Guru Arya. Megharoopan followed closely behind. He wanted to stop the rock before it hit the sanyasi's body. But, as though obeying an order, the rock stopped hurtling and halted in front of the sanyasi.

Megharoopan, who had sped all the way, placed a foot on top of the rock, and observed the sanyasi closely.

What? Did he have the power to make even rocks obey his command?

Megharoopan had no idea how long he stood there, staring at the sanyasi. When he came back to consciousness, he found himself lying prostrate, his forehead touching the mendicant's feet. He crouched to fit himself within the sanyasi's shadow as though it were a shade he had reached after trekking a long distance in a desert. Soon, two arms caressed him lovingly.

"Arise, son!"

He felt gratified, as though he had just heard the most melodious piece of music in the entire universe. On realising that he was experiencing ineffable joy, too superior even for his senses to transmit, he lay there and gazed up at the guru. He looked only once. But his eyes could not look on fixedly at that face.

It glows so fiercely!

"Arise, son!"

Megharoopan stood up as if in a dream. He usually held his head bent, but now he bowed even more. Looking into Guru Arya's eyes, Megharoopan asked, "Guru, who are you?"

The guru smiled and replied slowly, "I am all."

Megharoopan looked uncomprehendingly and curiously at the guru.

The guru asked him, "You didn't get it, did you?" Without waiting for Megharoopan's reply, the guru continued smilingly, "I am no-one."

Now, Megharoopan was utterly confused. He pleaded helplessly.

"Guru, I don't have the ability to understand who you are. So, you should tell me yourself. Also, please be kind enough to explain why you have come to a place that is full of sorrow and misery."

The guru appeared lost in thought for a while. Then, he replied, "You'll understand who I am, by and by." And he continued, "I've come here to put an end to the sorrow and misery you spoke of. I'm going to help all the people of this place escape all their sorrows and troubles."

On hearing that, Megharoopan stood bewildered.

Put an end to all the sorrows and suffering of all the people of this place? Will everyone be saved?

The guru's words sounded totally unimaginable to Megharoopan. There was only one way the residents of the saffron hill could overcome their plight and escape. That was through ascension to heaven. But for it to happen, one had to follow certain extremely austere rituals. This much, Megharoopan was sure of. The rituals had been followed meticulously through generations, but to no avail. The consequent disappointment had left him disenchanted. So, the guru's promise sounded attractive to his ears. He could not help responding.

"O Guru! I can't believe my ears! I wonder whether my senses are deceiving me. Are they? Please forgive me. Are you speaking the truth?"

The guru continued to smile. "Can a sanyasi utter anything simpler than the truth?"

Megharoopan was so overwhelmed that he bent over once again so his head touched Guru Arya's feet. He muttered, as though chanting the verses of a prayer, "Save us, Guru. Remove the shackles from our arms and feet!"

Megharoopan's ardent plea touched Guru Arya deeply. The guru raised Megharoopan to his feet and spoke in a loving voice.

"Where are your other humans?"

That was when Megharoopan returned to reality. He invited the guru.

"Please come with me. My humans are on this hill and in the garden on the hillslope. Please come."

As he led the guru, Megharoopan suddenly stopped, as though he had remembered something. He began to look in all directions.

The guru asked, "Who are you looking for?"

"Satyakan," said Megharoopan, sounding sad.

"Satyakan?" Guru Arya's voice was tinged with curiosity.

"Yes, Satyakan. My close friend. We were carrying the soil together. That was when I suddenly spotted you. I don't remember what happened after that. I wonder where he has gone."

It appeared to Guru Arya that Megharoopan had more to say. He patted Megharoopan on his shoulder and consoled him.

"Don't worry. Keep walking. He may be in the garden."

But Megharoopan continued to stand there, looking in four directions.

The guru's voice boomed in the sad-looking Megharoopan's ears once again, like a command.

"Walk on!"

Like a guilty child, Megharoopan started walking along with the guru.

THREE

As he climbed the hill, Guru Arya looked around. Humans were climbing the steep hill with great difficulty, carrying baskets of soil that were too heavy for them. On seeing them do this hard labour as a ritual, Guru Arya became at once anxious, astonished and sorrowful.

Why are these humans undertaking all this trouble?

No matter how hard he thought, Guru Arya could not crack the puzzle. He enquired to Megharoopan.

Looking into the infinite space beyond, Megharoopan whimpered, "This earth is full of saffron hills. At any given point in time, there are ten thousand and eleven people involved in these rituals on each one of them. The instruction is that as much clayey soil as possible should be dug up from the valley and taken to the top of the hill. This kind of sticky soil is found in abundance in the valley, and that is dug out from wells. One individual should dig only one well, and keep digging until water is sighted. But not a single well dug in the valley of the saffron hill has yielded any water so far. As a result, these humans have been digging the same wells all this while. And the work of carrying the soil up the hill has been going on without a break. Isn't it a strange thing? No matter how much soil we dig up, our wells do not become empty. We suspect that, unknown to us, someone is filling our wells with more of this soil instead of water. It is the same soil we carry up the hill. If we are able to transport all the soil to the crest of the hill, our mission will be accomplished. But no-one has been successful so far."

Then, looking around, he said as though sharing a secret, "You know what this soil is for? We are building a path to heaven!" He stopped for a brief moment to savour the inexplicable joy he felt, and continued, "Heaven lies on the other side of the clouds floating just above the saffron hill. If we pile more soil on the saffron hill and increase its height, we will be able to enter heaven easily. Heaven is a pleasure garden, untouched by death. There is no place for wrinkly old age, sadness, misery, ill health of the body or the mind, pain of separation, disappointment or troubles of poverty. And we have been doing these rituals with precision for such a long time, through many generations, in order to attain heaven."

Megharoopan continued, "By the time we reach halfway up the steep saffron hill with baskets of soil on our heads, most of us are invariably exhausted. The rest go up some more distance. But when it becomes impossible to reach the summit, they too take rest. However, by then the soil they had carried that far would have slipped down without their being aware of it. When they do realise it, they curse the fruitless exercise and withdraw themselves for the day. At that point, they are replaced by an equal number of humans. And the effort continues.

"The state of all the countless saffron hills on this earth is the same. The attempts to increase the height of the saffron hills go on all the time, here, there and everywhere. But the most mysterious fact is that none of us has seen the summit of the hill. It seems the instruction is that no-one should climb the hill without a basket of soil on their heads. This time, I had resolved to take my basket of soil to the intended spot. I must have reached the halfway mark when I saw you."

Guru Arya was trying to visualise the rigorous labour and unravel the mystery surrounding it.

Carrying insufferably heavy loads of soil on the head and climbing the steep hill in order to reach its peak! What a punishment, be it an instruction or part of a ritual!

Guru Arya became distraught. He asked Megharoopan, "Who told you that there is a heaven above the clouds on top of the hill?"

Megharoopan was quick to reply.

"That is our unconscious feeling."

Guru Arya laughed. "The heaven that you described – even that is your imagination?"

Megharoopan's eyes widened. "It's not a figment of imagination! Heaven is beyond all that! There, grains and pulses will discard their outer cover on their own and present themselves to be eaten. Tree branches, heaving with fruit, will bend low on seeing us, and humbly allow us to pluck whatever we want. Even tall trees will lower their branches. Their fruits are for our picking."

He continued enthusiastically, "There are streams of ambrosia in heaven. And rivers of milk and honey. They will flow close to us and invite us to scoop handfuls to drink."

As he kept on talking, Guru Arya asked in a serious tone, "Do you and your humans believe all this completely?"

Megharoopan's reply carried his strong conviction. "Indeed! We believe it! Isn't that why we are taking all this trouble? Is it for nothing that we carry so much soil up this steep saffron hill, and try to increase its height?"

Just as these strange beliefs and punishing labour began to haunt Guru Arya as mysterious phenomena, Megharoopan spoke aloud as though he had emerged from a dream.

"Here we are! The garden!"

The guru looked all around.

Where's the garden? With no leaves or flowers, how does this become a garden?

The guru looked to Megharoopan questioningly.

Understanding the significance of the glance, Megharoopan explained the great mystery. "This is indeed the garden, guru. Once upon a time, this was a garden full of fragrant flowers, luxuriant plants and luscious fruits. But sadly, a few powerful people plucked all the leaves and flowers, broke all the branches, and destroyed the garden. I have heard that those acts were not accidental ones but consciously executed operations of annihilation. After all, only if flowers and fruit available here were destroyed could those collected from bumper harvests elsewhere be brought over. As a result, small quantities of products brought from other places were given to us as wages at the end of the heavy labour done here. Those who were not happy with the situation tried to rebuild the garden here. But their attempts failed. Now, those efforts have been abandoned for fear that they will interfere with our digging wells and carrying soil. But there was a garden here a long while back. So, those of us who hold on to our old traditions continue to call it a garden."

The guru found the legend very fascinating. He laughed uproariously and asked, "But why did your efforts at creating a garden fail? Likewise, why didn't you plant saplings here once again? Why didn't you sow seeds?"

In total helplessness, Megharoopan replied, "What could we do? There was something else besides digging wells and hauling soil. Plants would grow in the saffron soil only once!"

Then, lowering his voice to a whisper, as though imparting a secret, he said, "Somebody, who is either controlling the saffron hill or inspiring us at the subconscious level to lug the soil and build the path to heaven, is standing in the way!"

He did not close the lid on the box of secrets. A few more secrets spilled out.

"It bothers me that those who are unable to dig wells or transport the soil cannot live on the saffron hill. Similarly, those with disabilities do not survive long here. Differently abled babies die either in infancy or during childhood. The state of women is another worrisome issue. Most baby girls die at birth. If you examine the current gender statistics, the ratio is invariably two or three men to one woman, on average.

It doesn't get any better than that! I have a strong feeling all this is a pre-planned, mysterious strategy designed by that hidden power, that formless, absent presence which controls the saffron hills."

"Are you the only one to feel that anxiety?" Guru Arya enquired.

The reply was quick.

"No. All of us have it. But—"

When Megharoopan hesitated to complete his reply, the guru goaded him.

"Speak up!"

Megharoopan said quickly, "Someone is blocking us at a subconscious level and preventing us from sharing our anxieties among ourselves."

Guru Arya understood the essence of his reply completely. Then, pretending to ignore his apprehension, the guru asked, "You said something in between, about saffron hill, didn't you?"

Megharoopan said, "Yes. This place where we are standing – this is a saffron hill."

The guru asked, "This is the place you call the saffron hill?"

"Yes," Megharoopan replied with conviction.

"What a pity!" The guru became angry all of a sudden. "Is this place that has gone red with your blood and tears – is this place a saffron hill? Isn't it outrageous that you chose the word 'saffron' to describe the colour of blood? Who named this soil 'saffron' when it has turned red with the blood of martyrs?"

The guru was panting hard. Megharoopan looked at him with concern.

What is the guru talking about?

"This is a blood hill! This soil has become red because your blood fell on it."

Megharoopan did not understand anything. But he did get

a vague sense of what the guru implied. But all he could do was stare at the guru with tear-filled eyes.

On seeing him upset, the guru said, "This is your earth. This soil has turned red because of your blood. You are being made to call it saffron hill, and you are being made to see it as *not* belonging to you by those very agents that you describe as powerful people, by those which your subconscious mind perceives as invisible powers, by those whom you consider formless beings!"

He continued, "The same holds true of this mirage called 'heaven'! First, you are made to raise the height of the hill so that it reaches the skies. For that, you are asked to carry headloads of soil from the valley right up to the summit of the hill. Soon, you will be ordered to build a path through the clouds at a great height. And that is named the 'heavenly path'. Don't you see it? You are made to believe that all the strange, impractical ideas and mysterious desires of your mind have a material existence, and you are deceived into believing that it is heaven!"

When he continued, his voice became stern sounding with rage.

"And a whole community is willing to swallow all this. Hook, line and sinker. And to undertake any amount of useless labour in the name of rituals!"

For some strange reason, the guru's angry tone caused Megharoopan to feel frightened. He felt an unfamiliar smell spreading, and dry wafts of wind blowing all around. An invisible form of a fragrant being seemed to ride on the wings of the wind.

On perceiving this, Megharoopan held the guru's hands within his firm clasp, and pleaded, "O Guru! Please be calm, please be calm!"

As Megharoopan continued to chant this like a mantra, the guru regained his equipoise. He stood in front of Megharoopan, serene as a great ocean on which the waves had been quelled.

After a long spell of silence, the guru asked, "Did I cause you pain, son? I spoke thoughtlessly!" Before waiting for a reply, he enquired, "Where are your humans? I need to see them."

Megharoopan felt relieved. He led the guru to the middle of the garden. "Please come," he said.

While walking, Megharoopan experienced, for the first time in his life, a deep sense of love towards the soil he trod on. Maybe he was influenced by the words uttered by Guru Arya about the earth just a few moments back. He, who had trained himself to say 'my humans' all this while, now began to feel the phrase 'my soil' trickle on his tongue.

Megharoopan accompanied the guru, muttering 'My humans, my soil' like a prayer.

FOUR

Megharoopan had said that the humans were resting. But Guru Arya did not feel it was true. He knew that taking rest was far more difficult for them than doing strenuous work.

Pointing to a wrinkled but healthy old man, Megharoopan said, "He is an old man. As soon as he is done with his rest, he will proceed either to carry soil or to dig the well."

Guru Arya felt distressed. He was about to remark that putting a venerable old man to hard labour was merciless torture. But before he could, Megharoopan pointed to an old woman. The guru, pre-empting his statement, asked, "She's an old woman, isn't she?"

Megharoopan nodded and said, "Yes."

Guru Arya looked at the old woman and realised she was waiting for someone. From time to time, she shaded her eyes with her hand, looked into the distance, and muttered something. It was obvious to the guru that she was expecting somebody. His mind began to grow restless.

Just then, pointing to a man and a middle-aged woman, who seemed completely lost in her sorrow, Megharoopan remarked, "Guru, they are a married couple. I don't know why they find it impossible to take rest, even for a minute."

The guru blurted, "Wonderful leisure time!"

As they walked further, they saw a young woman. She

appeared to be suppressing her dissatisfaction over having accepted something unwanted and feeling overwhelmed about it. Close by was a young man crouching in disappointment because he had failed to console her.

Only then did Megharoopan laugh. He muttered, "They are lovers. The young lady feels tormented for having indulged in youthful wantonness and transgressed certain limits. The man, on the other hand, feels bitter, suspecting he has lost a treasure that had just come to hand. But this conflict will last only a few minutes. As soon as their recess time is over, they'll get back to work – either lugging soil or digging the well. Of course, then, they'll forget all this."

The guru only smiled.

After they had walked some distance, they came across teenagers who, instead of skipping around in joy, sat with their heads between their knees.

Looking at them, Megharoopan remarked, "They are kids. There's nothing on the saffron hill to keep them entertained. And they can see that for themselves."

This was the first time that the guru was getting a glimpse of adolescents who looked totally dispirited. He did not gaze long at them. He paced forward.

After covering a great distance, he finally spotted the children of the saffron hill. They had lost their cloak of childhood and were wailing in hunger. The sight was so scorching that the guru could not take another step forward.

Sensing this, Megharoopan led the guru to a stone parapet nearby.

The guru tried to escape from the surrounding sights by withdrawing his eyes inward. But the whole scene revealed itself only all too clearly to his inner eye. He realised that each human he had encountered so far was not a specific individual. There were scores and scores of others behind them with similar faces. This situation was simply unendurable.

The guru jumped back to his feet, and said in a shivering voice, "Megharoopa, son. We cannot afford to wait any longer."

Caught momentarily in a surge of ecstasy, Megharoopan could not reply immediately. He was looking intently into the guru's eyes, which were glowing with compassion.

"Megharoopa, let's save your humans!" Guru Arya exclaimed enthusiastically. "I'm talking about a permanent escape. An eternal release from all sorrows and miseries."

FIVE

Guru Arya's words sent tremors all around the saffron hill, sweeping over the garden like a storm. Hearing them, the humans flocked towards Guru Arya, full of optimism.

What? Was there another way? To escape the sorrows and tribulations of this saffron hill? Towards heaven that was so excruciatingly difficult to reach or perhaps even inaccessible? Who was giving advice about this path?

These thoughts welled up in their minds as the people surrounded the guru.

Megharoopan announced, "My humans! This is the guru who has come to rescue us from all our troubles. He will lead us through a path that is different from the one of laborious tasks we have been following like a ritual so far."

All the people bowed their heads in front of Guru Arya.

Megharoopan continued, "The guru promises to release us immediately from all sorrows and all miseries."

The assembled people were at a loss for words. Long years of following the arduous and utterly fruitless ritual had converted them into walking images of sorrow and misery. They had completely lost hope. Kneeling on the ground, they stretched their empty hands towards the guru and pleaded.

Guru Arya's heart became fervent. He raised his arms and blessed the people. Then he asked Megharoopan, "Have all your humans reached here? May I disclose to them the escape route?"

Megharoopan replied, "Not all of them. Those who are bound to carry soil and dig wells are still engaged in the ritual. Let them come too."

"Alright. Please tell everyone to assemble in the garden at this time tomorrow. I shall instruct them on the path of liberation."

Megharoopan announced the guru's instruction to the people.

"My humans! Everyone belonging to this saffron hill should be present here at this hour tomorrow. Our guru will advise us on how to free ourselves."

The people turned ecstatic. Their faces looked remarkably similar to one another, masked over by forgetfulness regarding their current plight.

Megharoopan too was riding the crest of joy. He soon joined the crowd.

"This is our last night on the saffron hill that has given us untold sorrow and troubles. Let us curse this night. Let us shred it to pieces. But never mind! Let's do something else. Let's all remain awake this whole night and watch it pass. Or maybe we should go to sleep. A sleep to end wakefulness, once and for all. Or, better still, a sleep towards the final awakening."

The crowd was beside themselves with joy.

The guru called Megharoopan. "Come with me. Let me speak to you in private."

Megharoopan was ready to join the guru, but suddenly, as if remembering something, he looked around searchingly.

"What are you looking for?"

"Satyakan," Megharoopan replied sadly.

"He may be here somewhere. You come with me."

But when Megharoopan appeared to hesitate, the guru insisted, "Come."

Finally, as though pulled by some invisible power, Megharoopan began to follow the guru's shadow.

SIX

The humans lay on the ground in the garden. Even as they remained awake, they were reluctant to talk to one another. All of them were caught in their own private worlds, in the sky-worlds of their minds.

A sanyasi from some place has come here. And he promises us release from all troubles. How on earth did he realise that we had willed ourselves to work incessantly and hard all this while, precisely for the sake of freedom? Hadn't all the previous generations been yoked to this very same back-breaking work? All those efforts have been utterly purposeless. This is the first time we've seen hope right in front of us! Maybe this will work!

When thoughts ran wild, the old man could no longer contain himself. He spoke to the countless other old men lying in a row next to him.

"The sanyasi may be a divine person. He may know some mantras."

A wave of murmurs swept over the row. Then, as if uttering a prayer, they spoke in unison.

"That's likely. That's likely."

An old woman, who lay hearing everything, spoke in a shivering voice to those in her row, "What about us?"

A reply was heard immediately. Someone in the row said, "He must be the one!"

The old woman felt consoled.

Hearing their sigh of relief, the middle-aged couple wove their dreams.

What could he possibly have in store for us? Maybe he'll help us dissolve into each other!

When their middle-aged laughter spread mysteriously into the row of the youths, the young men and women became more restive. As far as they were concerned, they had reached a midpoint in their journey, equidistant from both ends. Besides, their youth was not one given to weaving dreams about physical reality.

All this while, the adolescents of the saffron hill were eagerly waiting for interesting adventures. And the infants, sucking their still-to-mature fingers, in true childlike fashion, looked at the garden with curiosity.

SEVEN

Resting his head on Megharoopan's lap in the garden, fragrant with absent flowers, Guru Arya asked, "Son, what do you feel?"

"Divine revelation... satisfaction... gratification." Megharoopan spoke as though in a dream.

The guru, feeling happy, asked wonderingly, "Really?"

Megharoopan replied, "Really!"

EIGHT

Forgetting all his other emotions, Guru Arya took pity on the earth that had grown tired, enduring the solar flares, the endless rotation and the revolution along the orbit.

Inner turmoil is more insufferable than anything else. Subjection to relentless abuse will turn anyone into a worshipper of sorrow.

Understanding this truth, Guru Arya addressed the earth, "O Vasundhara! Your fate is a similar one. I have put an end to all my feelings of enmity towards you. I am filled with compassion for you."

Observing the guru's face growing flushed with ardour, Megharoopan asked, "What's happening, guru?"

"Everything!"

Megharoopan did not understand the point. But he tried hard not to cause any displeasure to the guru with further questions.

The guru went into deep meditation. Megharoopan felt the guru was using his heart to console somebody. He was not sure what it was. After a long while, his restlessness became palpable to the guru.

Guru Arya asked, "Megharoopan, do you have any idea how I am going to save your humans? If you don't, how is it that you have no questions for me?"

Megharoopan gave a reply immediately.

"I have faith in you. That feeling sprouted the moment I caught a glimpse of you for the first time. I'm sure you'll show us a way to escape. But that path need not be revealed exclusively to me. I'm interested in learning about it only along with the rest of my humans."

The guru felt immeasurable respect for Megharoopan. He asked again, "Aren't you curious to learn about it? Even a little?"

"No, Guru." Megharoopan was categorical. "I have no wish whatsoever to be the only one to hear it."

"Not even a bit?"

"Not even the least bit!"

NINE

The waves of the great human sea that had converged in the garden subsided. Everyone perked up their ears. Megharoopan felt this was the calm before the storm. And, as if to confirm it, a scene played itself out just then. The ten thousand and eleven people who had been entrusted with the task of carrying soil up the hill, and those expected to dig wells, came together to the garden. The sea of humans experienced a momentary upsurge.

Megharoopan feared whether uncontrollable waves would begin to swell.

Such a thing has never happened at the saffron hill! – there is no-one to carry soil! Besides, those assigned the task of digging their wells have abandoned their duty. Will the powers, that have been controlling us invisibly, remain calm? All humans are sitting idle at the same time.

The saffron hill residents, who had always and steadfastly upheld the tradition, felt their hearts break into a million pieces.

This should not be happening! Everyone is inactive! The ritual of digging wells and carrying soil, that had begun aeons back, has suffered a break! What is going to happen now?

They became fearful.

Then, out of the blue, a divine presence that could drive away all fears and anxieties, made his appearance in the garden.

Guru Arya and Megharoopan walked into the garden. The people stopped talking, forgot everything, and with bated breath, cocked their ears to listen to the life-saving sermon.

TEN

Even as he entered the garden as Guru Arya's shadow, Megharoopan's heart bore a heavy burden of personal sorrow. It was as if some vague sense of uneasiness had reached a flash point and begun to crackle and burn in the fireplace in the middle of that burden. Until then, he had endured only sorrows and troubles. But now, Megharoopan realised, his state of mind was different. Far different from what it had been earlier – and it made him intensely uncomfortable.

Guru Arya divined his uneasiness. In fact, he had been focusing on Megharoopan all the time. When he felt that Megharoopan was not even conscious they had entered the garden, the guru touched him, "Son…"

As though awakened from sleep, Megharoopan responded, "What is it, guru?"

"We have reached the garden."

"Please forgive me, guru," Megharoopan replied in all humility. "I was virtually sleepwalking. I was thinking of something and walking in a daze."

The guru stopped on his tracks, and asked, "What's disturbing you?"

Megharoopan replied without any hesitation. "We have been waiting through generations to hear the liberty sermon, and at this moment, at this rare and auspicious hour, I do not see my Satyakan."

The guru paid keen interest to Megharoopan as he continued.

"We have always been inseparable friends. But ever since you came here, guru, I've not seen him. In fact, I forgot him, caught up as I was in intoxicating thoughts about escape!"

The guru tried to console him. "Your Satyakan has not gone anywhere," he said. Then, he quickly glanced all around, and pointing in one direction, remarked, "There stands your Satyakan!"

Megharoopan's eyes darted in the direction pointed to by the guru's finger.

Yes. That is indeed Satyakan! He is standing away from the crowd. He alone!

Megharoopan shouted involuntarily, "Satyaka! Satyaka!"

But when Megharoopan attempted to clear a way for himself, pushing the sea of humans to the sides, Guru Arya stopped him.

"Wait! It's not time yet."

ELEVEN

Walking to the shade of an absent Ashoka tree in the garden, Guru Arya surveyed the assembly. It was a virtual sea of humans without borders which stretched right up to the horizon. However, the vastness had a peculiarity. The front row was occupied by those whose faces differed according to their age. But behind each individual were countless others with the same facial features. When he remembered that all of them were awaiting his words about the path towards liberation, Guru Arya unconsciously addressed them.

"My humans!"

The crowd responded in a tone of humility that was laced with subservience. The guru was transported to a level of super divine bliss. It felt as though he was being carried away by a pure stream of intoxication that had flowed past ancient generations.

Picking up a fistful of sand from the ground, and rubbing it between his palms, the guru spoke with devotional fervour.

"My soil! My dear Vasundhara! Please understand that I have no feelings of hostility towards you. I am going to liberate these humans whom you have held prisoner."

He stopped for a moment and then continued, "My effort is not to make you lonely. All I desire is to release these humans from their sorrows and tribulations."

The crowd looked on with interest, watching every move of the guru. They were completely captivated by what they saw and eagerly awaited his divine words.

The guru came out quickly, very quickly, from his meditative trance, and, casting off all tender emotions, adopted a serious mien. The crowd held their breath in order to take in the flow of ethereal words that was about to slip out of his lips.

"My humans..." The guru addressed them. "There is only one way to liberty, and that is *Mrityusutra!*"

He stopped, gathered power from the infinite space, and continued, "Forget your proposition about ascension to heaven. It was nothing but an impractical and idiotic exercise. I have forgiven the invisible ones who promised you entry into heaven if you agreed to dig wells in the valley, carry the clayey soil up the steep hill, lay it over the crest to increase its height, and then build a skywalk through the clouds to heaven. I have forgiven you too who believed that tenet and sacrificed your entire life. Adopt the right path, at least now!"

The guru's language soon acquired a prophet's register.

"If sorrows and suffering are to come to an end, they have to disappear. But sorrows and suffering in the lives of humans are as unshakeable as the redness of their blood. They will remain until the last puff of air they breathe and the last drop of blood they hold. It is only when blood and breath stop that sorrows and suffering will end. Such a state can be brought into being only by *Mrityusutra*. We have to create for ourselves a time that is out of sync with Nature, and thus escape. That is the secret of *Mrityusutra*."

By the time he finished speaking, the dam inside the depths of the guru's soul burst. The floodwaters inside him surged uncontrollably. Thereafter, he could not utter a word. He stood there silently... for a minute, two minutes, several minutes...

After a long time, the crowd stirred a little.

When Megharoopan spied the winds of restlessness sweep over the great sea of humans, he became terribly agitated. Though hesitantly, he touched Guru Arya with great humility, and told him, "O Guru! I don't understand what *Mrityusutra* means. Can you explain it in simple terms?"

Guru Arya laughed. It lasted only a minute. He became silent again. Then, he began to speak in a tender voice, "All of you are gross and subtle aspects of the infinite. Right now, the timeless infinite has extended its compassionate arms of *Paramananda* or ultimate bliss into the space that separates you from your true self. It summons you. The biggest obstacle that you need to understand and overcome is the distance that keeps you away from the real you.

"Some people require only a minute to achieve it. Others use up their entire lifetime. If you become aware of *Paramananda*, or if you can imagine what the experience of ultimate bliss means, you will accept it."

Without waiting for any response from the people, he continued, "It's unlikely that there's any living creature that does not desire *Paramananda*. Do you know what *Paramananda* is?"

Guru Arya stopped and said, as though sharing a secret, "That is an inner state. A blissful condition of joy that outmatches all joys!"

The rest of his speech was explanatory. His words blew like the wind towards the ears of the saffron hill residents.

"Happiness and *Paramananda* are intoxicating experiences that are unique to each individual. Likewise, the path towards attaining them is unique. A few find them in wealth, good fortune and authority. Some, in alcohol, religious devotion or other inebriating substances. Others, in orgasm during love games with their favourite person. Thus, the factors that cause *Paramananda* are numerous, and the ecstasy they bring you may last minutes, days, years or perhaps an entire lifetime. That is *Paramananda*. That state of ultimate bliss can be created by you personally. And that is yours to keep. It summons you always, now and forever. Don't you have the desire to acquire it? Tell me!"

"Yes, yes!"

The crowd spoke in one voice. Guru Arya felt jubilant.

"I am talking precisely about the path leading to it. That is *Mrityusutra*." After a moment's pause, he resumed, "All of us live in fearful anticipation of that split second when the life spark leaves us. We wait until Nature creates that moment for us. But what we are going to do here is simply this – we will create that moment for ourselves. We create a moment that is not designated by Nature, return our life independently, become a blessed part of the infinite, and reach that insuperable position. Thereafter, there is no life or death. Only bliss, *Paramananda*, ultimate bliss!"

The people were still in a state of bewilderment. They were overwhelmed. Understanding their dilemma, the guru spoke more lucidly.

"All of us lead our lives awaiting the moment of death. Our liberation lies there. Only there! In death alone! Isn't death inevitable? Won't we die at some point of time? That said, why should we undergo so many difficulties and continue to live till that time? Why should we endure so much trouble, eating and drinking, sometimes going hungry and thirsty too, suffering pain and inflicting it too? In any case, we have to die, one day or another. That being so, why not die now itself?"

Looking into the infinite distance, he continued, "Do you know what a pleasurable experience death is? It is an enticing form of oblivion. After death, we become a celestial aspect of the infinite. After death, we will enjoy ineffable, unsurpassable bliss, exclusively. *Mrityusutra* is the only path towards *Paramananda*."

What flowed out of Guru Arya were meditative sounds.

"So, let's give ourselves up. Let's die before Nature snatches life from us. Let's create that moment for ourselves as quickly as possible. Let's escape by seeking death. There's liberty in this universe only through death. That is the ultimate truth."

The people were fully convinced by the time Guru Arya

reached the end of his exhaustive commentary. Waves of relief rose and fell on the sea of humans.

Megharoopan blinked his eyes as though he had seen pure, divine light. He prostrated himself in front of the guru and said, "I'm blessed, having listened to the ultimate principle of *Mrityusutra*. I'm convinced there is no path of escape other than the one you have revealed. My humans too, desire to reach that ultimate bliss after having listened to your truth."

The guru laughed on hearing it. After some time, he told Megharoopan, "You must grind this nugget of truth too against a whetstone. Let your humans consider whether *Mrityusutra* is entirely acceptable to them."

On hearing that, Megharoopan became peeved.

"O Guru! I feel you have doubts about us. We know that there is no truth above what your words have conveyed. And yet, you think we should mull over it?"

"Indeed, Megharoopa."

Stroking Megharoopan, the guru said, "The arguments favouring and opposing the last judgement of your humans are contained within this very principle. So, introspection is of great relevance here. Let everyone give it considerable thought. If the decision is a unanimous one, I shall be the master of ceremonies and lead them to the ultimate bliss."

On hearing the guru's explanation, Megharoopan felt it was right.

Let each individual's right – to think about their final judgement before taking a final decision – remain a fundamental one.

Megharoopan looked at the people. They continued to lie prostrate on the ground. Directing them to rise, he said, "We, who were lucky enough to listen to *Mrityusutra*, should decide whether or not to seek our escape through that ultimate truth."

By the time he finished his statement, the crowd chanted raucously, "We want to escape, we want to escape".

Yet Megharoopan continued, "You should not make up your mind as soon as you hear something. Let's spend the rest of the day thinking about it. Then, after arriving at a decision, let's assemble here at this same hour tomorrow. If our decision is unanimous, the guru has promised to open the doors for our escape, be a witness to it, and even officiate at the ceremony."

As he said this, Megharoopan suddenly remembered Satyakan. The reason was that he wondered what his own decision in the matter was. Until that day, Megharoopan had never taken any decision on his own or independently. He had always consulted Satyakan. But now... He felt he was committing a grievous sin.

Is it possible to do anything on my own, without Satyakan?

Megharoopan began to analyse the issue himself. He had to see Satyakan.

Where's Satyakan? No decision is possible without consulting him! Can he be here somewhere?

Megharoopan peered into the dispersing crowd.

No! Satyakan is not among them!

He looked in all four directions.

No! Satyakan is nowhere to be seen!

Observing Megharoopan's growing sense of apprehension, Guru Arya said, "Megharoopa, you should go too."

The guru turned and walked away.

Megharoopan called after him, "Where are you going, guru?"

"Nowhere. Yet everywhere!"

The reply sent Megharoopan into the abyss of confusion, but he pretended to have understood it. His mind was turbulent with roiling thoughts about Satyakan.

It's imperative that I find Satyakan.

Megharoopan began to walk aimlessly.

TWELVE

The humans of the saffron hill were in a state of confused wonderment.

The day of liberation will dawn tomorrow! That means release from all miseries. Journey towards the pinnacle of bliss. Paramananda!

They forgot that the tradition had been violated. They forgot their saffron hill. Their minds and dreams were full of *Paramananda*!

THIRTEEN

The first night at the saffron hill when neither wells were dug nor soil carried up. The first night at the saffron hill that had lost its work-awareness. The first night at the saffron hill when no-one recognised the other.

But there was one person at the saffron hill who knew everything. A person unknown to Megharoopan, Guru Arya or Satyakan. And behind him, were countless others who looked just like him!

FOURTEEN

Megharoopan was uneasy. Even while savouring the prospect of experiencing *Paramananda* in a short while, he was disturbed by the thought that crores and crores of humans of the saffron hill were being coaxed towards death. Death by suicide. He stood shivering as though he were a lone traveller who had lost his way and was trapped amidst wild animals in a dense forest in the dead of night.

Surely, I am not the one abetting my humans to commit suicide!

That feeling gave him some relief. But the role he played in it gnawed at his heart whenever the thought struck him. He did not have the courage even to imagine what would happen at the saffron hill the next day. He ardently wished Satyakan were with him.

That will be such a consolation. Satyakan has a solution for anything and everything.

Despite his firm conviction regarding the correctness of his act, Megharoopan could not understand why his mind was wavering.

Satyakan has the ability to calm even the most turbulent mind. But where is he?

When Megharoopan remembered that he had neither seen Satyakan anywhere at close quarters nor talked to him ever since he met the guru, he felt his heart break. Blood began to ooze, and the bruise started hurting.

I must see Satyakan.

Megharoopan's heart throbbed hard.

I cannot afford to lose him.

Megharoopan began to walk, calling out Satyakan's name like a chant, as though he were possessed.

FIFTEEN

Megharoopan's feet ached, having climbed up and down the hills and wandered in the valleys. His body grew tired, having swum along streams and in lakes.

Where? Where is my Satyakan?

He went on wailing.

Finally, when he entered the Arya forest, he could no longer endure the pain. Looking at the silent bamboo clumps, he asked, "O copse! O bamboo copse! Did you see my Satyakan?"

The bamboo stalks did not even whistle in reply.

Megharoopan walked deep into the forest, but he did not notice the forest at all. He did not see the climbers full of blooming flowers. He did not hear the gigantic trees covered over by the climbers, whimpering on spotting him.

He asked the flowers, and the climbers that held them, "Did you see my Satyakan?"

None of them gave him even a fragrant clue in reply.

He asked the shady trees and the sky, "Did you see my Satyakan?"

None of them uttered even a single word in reply.

He asked the wind and the sunrays, "Did you see my Satyakan?"

They did not pay him any attention.

Although none of them uttered anything about Satyakan, Megharoopan continued to ask about his friend to everyone and everything he saw.

Eventually, having lost his voice, with no energy left to either make gestures or move his limbs, and caught in an insufferable moral dilemma, Megharoopan collapsed deep in the woods. Even then, his heart throbbed, calling out, "Satyaka! Satyaka!"

SIXTEEN

Guru Arya looked at the earth as she continued to roll on the orbit-floor, cursing the sun and the entire solar system.

"O Vasundhara! There is a punishment for every crime!" Then he whispered to her, "When you ran away from the sun, did you realise how much pain you caused him? He had held you in the core of his heart. So, didn't you deserve a fitting punishment? And see, you got it!"

It appeared as if the earth was grievously wounded by Guru Arya's words. He noticed that her blood-shot eyes and customary fierce look had become piteous.

Guru Arya felt compassionate towards the earth and enraged with the sun.

"O Sun! Should the punishment be so severe? Did you notice what the earth did when the intensity of self-torture became too much for her to bear? She cursed all the humans who took birth in her womb! As a result, they are chained to eternal sorrow and suffering. The punishment meted out by the earth on the humans is insufferable pain and extremely rigorous work!"

After looking at the sun silently for a long time, Guru Arya spoke in a stern tone.

"O Sun! I am going to rescue all these humans. The earth will become lonely after that. How long will she be able to remain alone? O Sun! The earth has been waiting all this while for you to show pity. Won't you relent at least now?"

Guru Arya stood on the big toe of a single foot, raised his hands high above his head, and pleaded on the earth's behalf.

Eventually, he opened his eyes on hearing a whimpering sound. And what he saw was the earth withdrawing herself into the depths of her soul, singing a plaintive song.

"Please don't cry!" Guru Arya pleaded with the earth. "My effort is not to make you lonely. I only desire to save these humans."

Thereafter, he did not look at the earth for long. He feared that seeing her sad and silent demeanour he would have second thoughts. Instead, he focused all his thoughts on his main aim – the cleansing rites scheduled for the next day.

The escape of all humans on the earth! The rescue of all of them! What a holy act!

SEVENTEEN

Guru Arya was in a state of great joy. His slow gait resembled that of a sleepwalker. But when he suddenly remembered this was the last day that human odour would waft across the earth, he started. Then he consoled himself. He had taken upon himself the task of conducting a great ritual in the full conviction that it was totally right. Therefore, there was no room for remorse.

He searched for the essence of the truth in the depths of his soul. And what he heard in reply were musical notes of pure joy.

All truths are contained in 'Om', the primeval and eternal, generative sound. Even the essence of all arguments is dissolved as divine elements in it.

Guru Arya consoled himself by attempting an interpretation of his own ritualistic principles.

Justice and injustice are relative. What looks correct from the perspective of a viewer constitutes his justice. And what appears wrong is deemed injustice.

He went over it mentally, several times.

When he was absolutely sure all his decisions and acts were totally correct, Guru Arya slowed his pace. He looked around slowly. That was when he realised he had wandered into the Arya forest.

And then, a totally unexpected sight appeared before his eyes. Megharoopan was lying on the ground like an orphan!

The guru kneeled close to Megharoopan. When he caressed Megharoopan's body, he realised that the long search had exhausted Megharoopan. Megharoopan had been frantically searching for Satyakan and collapsed in sheer fatigue. Poor man! He was drained, looking in vain for his soul mate.

Guru Arya felt compassion for Megharoopan. He ordered the all-pervading wind to find out where Satyakan was and inform Megharoopan of his whereabouts.

Stroking Megharoopan fondly once more, the guru told the wind once again, "O wind! Don't make him weep!"

EIGHTEEN

An all-too-familiar smell penetrated his nostrils. At that moment, Megharoopan was in the middle of a dream in which he was engaged in sensual frolics with nude *Nagakanyas* in Lord Kama's love arbour which was studded with yellow blooms. It was an odour of someone very close to him.

Isn't it Satyakan's scent?

Megharoopan took a deep breath. Suddenly he realised the truth.

Indeed! This is distinctly Satyakan's!

Megharoopan woke up from his sleep with a start. He shouted like one possessed, "Satyaka! Satyaka!"

No-one in the forest, except the forest itself, heard his call. By then, Satyakan's scent had pervaded everywhere.

Megharoopan called the wind and wept.

"O wind! O wind! Where did you pick up this aroma from? This is my Satyakan's scent. Show me the way, won't you? Lead me towards Satyakan's scent!"

The wind, unsure of how to respond, stood startled for a minute. Then, it blew hard in one direction.

Megharoopan walked along the path indicated by the wind. When Satyakan's scent felt very strong at the mouth of a cave, the wind suddenly went still. Then it gradually withdrew itself into the cave.

Megharoopan understood the message.

Satyakan is inside!

He rushed into the cave like a surge that is released after being blocked for a while. He searched here and there inside the dark cave. Eventually, he saw Satyakan sleeping, with his arms wrapped around the glowing body of a nude woman. Megharoopan was shocked.

Gayathri! Our lady love!

Consumed with rage, Megharoopan forgot everything else. A treasure that was meant to be enjoyed equally by both had been usurped completely and exclusively by one! Who could tolerate this?

Megharoopan suppressed his fuming anger for a minute.

Satyakan was never like this! When the traditions were disrupted, when the thread of customs and rituals at the saffron hill was cut, did the roots of righteousness and moral practices too get severed?

Megharoopan's anger turned to sorrow. For the first time, he regretted having violated the traditions. He went into self-flagellation. But all this lasted only a short while. The very next minute, an unfamiliar and vague sense of indifference enveloped him. He looked dispassionately at Satyakan who had entered Gayathri. Then, unknown to himself, a cry from inside his soul issued out through his lips.

"Satyaka!"

Though slowly, the name echoed and re-echoed inside the cave. It did not subside for a long time. In fact, the echoes only multiplied as Megharoopan waited. He felt terrified. Then, in sheer confusion, he called out once again.

"Satyaka!"

This time, Satyakan woke up. Gayathri too. Their nude bodies swayed in the darkness. Satyakan's mind shook even more. He sounded utterly crushed when he asked Megharoopan,

"You... you...? How did you come here?"

Megharoopan continued to stare at Satyakan, without

bothering to reply. Satyakan's face was taken over by hatred and contempt. His movements appeared restless.

Megharoopan lamented inwardly.

What has happened to him? What a change has overcome him! Where is that soft and noble Satyakan of mine? Who's this terrible man?

"Didn't you hear my question? Why have you come here? And how did you reach this place?"

Megharoopan woke up from his thoughts on hearing Satyakan's harsh words. He called out ardently, "Satyaka!"

Although he got no reply, Megharoopan spoke, "Satyaka, I was wandering in search of you. I need to speak to you. We have to take a decision about the saffron hill and also about our humans. I came here for that."

"*How* did you come here? First tell me that! Who told you that you'd find me here?"

When Satyakan erupted in anger, Megharoopan opened his heart.

"The wind that wandered all over this garden, savouring your scent, saw my desperation, took pity on me, and showed me the way."

Satyakan felt he could not tolerate either seeing Megharoopan or listening to his words. And wasn't it the wind that revealed the path? Satyakan felt he had to take revenge on the wind. Blind with fury, he hollered, "Hey, wind!"

Gayathri understood the situation. She grabbed Satyakan's hand that had been raised to curse the wind, and said, "Like you, the omnipresent wind is a *satyakaami*, a lover of truth. It does not know how to tell untruths."

Satyakan became a bit calmer.

Stroking his arm that he had lowered, Gayathri said, "Control your anger. Isn't he too my lover? In that sense, aren't you both one?"

Satyakan seemed somewhat mollified. Seeing this, Megharoopan asked, "Satyaka, why this distance between us?

What crime did I commit? Why are you avoiding me? Why do you hate me so?"

Satyakan could no longer contain himself. He fumed, "You destroyed our tradition! You broke the rituals at the saffron hill! You stopped the work on the bridge to heaven!"

He continued his litany of Megharoopan's faults.

"You obstructed the digging of wells, the scooping and transport of the soil, and even the elevation of the saffron hill! In this manner, you struck at the very roots of our moral practices. All said and done, what you did was to stand in the way of our ascension to heaven!"

After a pause but with barely suppressed disappointment, he continued, "Didn't you become a follower of some magician, without having a word with me? Do you have any love for me? For the saffron hill? For our humans? Worse still, didn't you completely forget Gayathri?"

Megharoopan found it difficult to reply immediately. He took in Satyakan's questions and mulled over them.

What resistance can I offer? Was it my fault that I sought to rescue our humans of the saffron hill? I had only their best interests in mind. I did only good deeds and I am still doing only good things. Yet...

Megharoopan could not hold himself together. He asked, "Satyaka, did you even observe what I have been doing? I am rescuing everyone! Is that wrong?"

"Whom are you rescuing?" Satyakan shouted.

"I am rescuing every human on the saffron hill, including you, Gayathri and myself. With the blessings of the guru, we will embrace *Mrityusutra* and enjoy *Paramananda*."

Satyakan was beside himself with anger.

"Who is this guru of yours? And where is your *Paramananda*? You see *Paramananda* beyond death from where there is no return, isn't that so? Whoever knows that joy can be experienced there? What if that place is more hellish than this one?"

Megharoopan could not stand it anymore.

"I have adopted the path of truth."

"What if it's a fake one?" Satyakan countered. "Did you conduct experiments to confirm that your path is right? Has anyone who has experienced it endorsed the path? Did you discuss it with anyone?"

Megharoopan blasted out, "In that case, let me ask you something. Have you seen heaven? Will it have all the conveniences we enjoy here? Do you know anyone who has been there? Has anyone told us anything about it?"

Seeing Satyakan tongue-tied, Megharoopan persisted, "Our ancestors and all of us have worked really hard, digging wells in the valley of the saffron hill, collecting clayey soil, and taking it up the steep ascent, all in the hope of adding to its height, building a skywalk through the clouds, and entering heaven. And what has been the result? Has anyone gained access to heaven?"

The questions erupted from Megharoopan as though out of a box of puzzles and carried mysteries within them.

He went on, "Have you ever spotted water in any of the wells we have dug in the valley of the saffron hill? Doesn't the instruction demand that we continue to dig the wells until water trickles out? In spite of gouging out wells, and removing all the clayey soil they contain, who's filling them with fresh soil?"

Eventually, in utter hopelessness, he said, "These mysteries suffocate me. My dear Satyaka! I have only you to discuss this with. But ever since I saw the guru, you have been avoiding me. How then can I have a discussion?"

Although Satyakan had relented a little, the mention of the word 'guru' raised his hackles once again. He asked angrily, "Who's this guru of yours?"

Megharoopan replied with pride, "My guru is a saviour. He has advised us that the only escape route lies in embracing death through *Mrityusutra*. I believe that is absolutely true. The earlier we accept it, the quicker we will enjoy *Paramananda*."

Satyakan contested the point. Megharoopan spelt out his justifications once again.

As arguments and counterarguments went on, Gayathri felt they would not bode well for anyone of them. Holding their hands, she said, "All I hear inside this cave are echoes. Let's go out."

On hearing her suggestion, Satyakan walked out. Megharoopan followed and Gayathri walked in the middle. As soon as they came outside, Megharoopan's words echoed the throbs of his heart.

"Satyaka, I came in search of you for courage and support. To this day, have we taken any decision on our own, without consulting each other? Whatever I have said has been your decision too, and whatever you have said has been my decision as well. It must be the same in this case too. That's my wish."

Satyakan's heart melted on hearing that. He stopped walking and turned to look at Megharoopan. Megharoopan continued to speak.

"Satyaka, I am doing what I consider right. Just think about it! Why are we leading such a burdensome life, digging wells that yield no water, and carrying loads of soil whose weight is unbearable? Don't we all live only until the moment of death? The earlier we reach that moment, the faster we become a divine part of the infinite. There is joy in it. There is *Paramananda*."

Having said this much, Megharoopan looked at Satyakan with eager anticipation. Then he asked, "Is it wrong to wish well for our humans who are toiling so hard? Tell me, Satyaka. What I'm doing is absolutely right, isn't it?"

Megharoopan's words overpowered Satyakan. Eventually, after giving it considerable thought, Satyakan responded.

"Megharoopan, maybe what you say is true. But only to yourself!"

Megharoopan could not bear it. He asked, "Satyaka, is there a truth exclusively for me? We have never had differing opinions on anything so far, have we? Isn't that what I'm reminding you of?"

Satyakan stood rooted on the spot. Suddenly he felt an unfamiliar fragrance seep into the air all around. A dry puff of wind blew. An invisible, fragrant form riding the wings of the wind seemed threatening to him. Satyakan felt that the dry waft of wind and the invisible fragrant presence astride it had all along been giving him a vague impression right from the beginning that Megharoopan's thoughts, words and deeds were absolutely wrong. They continued to forbid Satyakan from agreeing with Megharoopan – and the ban appeared inviolable. It seemed to remind him of the repercussions of discontinuing the rituals at the saffron hill. Although he could not see or hear it, he could experience the invisible ban intensely.

Satyakan had no idea who was sounding the ban by resorting to persuasion and threats. All he knew was that either the arid wind or the fragrance riding on it was issuing instructions regarding someone's demands, in very clear and accurate terms. But Satyakan could not differentiate between them. He felt that the invisible presence of the fragrant figure astride the wind kept on reminding him of the many inducements that had worked behind the tough activities of the digging of dry wells and the transportation of soil to the top of the hill. The inducements had ranged from food to clothes, shelter to workplace and medicine to weapons. And within a split second, Satyakan was somehow made to feel convinced that these were not mere impressions but palpable realities.

He suddenly remembered that earlier too, he had felt the same. When he had refused to be by Megharoopan's side before the guru entered the garden, the barren wind as well as the fragrant figure atop it had sounded a whistle of threat in his ears. Now Satyakan was sure the threats were not imagined ones but real possibilities.

The dry wind unravelled before Satyakan the threatening

truth about hunger – a feeling appeased immediately after eating, yet one that gnaws at the insides a little while later. Food is necessary. But for food to be produced, farmlands, seeds and manure are required. And all the three entities are under the control of the fragrant figure riding the wind. Then the invisible power whispered yet another truth – as nudity causes feelings of shame, clothing is also essential. However, its attractiveness can always be improved. Shelter, too, is essential for sleeping, mating, creating the next generation and rearing it. But this demands money and buildings which can be acquired only with the help of farmlands and workplaces – both of which are also within the control of this power.

As though conveying a divine secret, the invisible power also informed Satyakan that anything can be used as a weapon. Even affection, love and lust! We can attract and defeat an adversary using care and compassion. Thus, leniency is also a weapon. Whatever we see or handle is a weapon – a weapon that can be used for anything and everything.

All the bans had been put in place by driving the threat into the subconscious mind. The threat of dire and unpredictable consequences if the traditions at the saffron hill – digging of dry wells and carrying of soil to increase the height of the hill – were either altered or defied. Satyakan had no doubts whatsoever of the reality of the warnings.

But it was not possible for him to say anything unpleasant to either Megharoopan or Gayathri. Either then or now. So, he kept everything to himself. He suppressed all his feelings and remained mute.

Megharoopan, divining this, said, "Something's bothering you. Whatever it be, spill it out. Let me get to know what your thoughts are."

Satyakan opened up.

"I am frightened. There's an invisible power and an unfamiliar odour here. I feel a dry whiff of wind and hear a fragrant rider preventing some things."

"That's nothing!" Megharoopan said categorically.

"My feelings constitute what is right for me. They have never gone wrong! Ever!" Satyakan continued in a distressed manner, "Some power, that controls us and the destiny of the saffron hill, is behind all this. I fear it is an invisible power that is unknown to us."

Megharoopan did not think it was a problem at all. Gathering self-confidence from some source, he remarked, "There's nothing that surpasses death, Satyaka. We are moving towards it. So, what's there to fear?"

Satyakan suddenly asked, "You are saying that all of us should die, aren't you?"

"Yes. You, Gayathri, myself, and all the humans of the saffron hill."

Satyakan looked as though he were about to burst into tears. "If we die, how will we be able to see Gayathri? How will we see the saffron hill? Hadn't you yourself said there can't be life for us without either Gayathri or the saffron hill?"

Megharoopan broke into a peal of laughter. "After death, is there life at all, Satyaka?"

Gayathri, who had walked ahead a little distance, heard their laughter, and asked joyously, "Have you mended fences so quickly? And started laughing together too?"

It was Megharoopan who replied, "Whenever we have spoken about you, we have only laughed."

Gayathri's curiosity was piqued. "What's there to speak about me now?"

Megharoopan gradually walked towards her. His body grazed against her fragrant figure. Resting his fingers gently on her soft shoulders, and looking deep into her eyes, that were like pools of love, he whispered into her ears, "Didn't you hear the guru talk about accepting *Mrityusutra* so that we can escape the sufferings at the saffron hill?"

She nodded.

"So, we are taking the route of death to reach *Paramananda*. 'If we embrace death in order to achieve that, how will we be able to see you?' That's Satyakan's worry!"

As he was saying this, Megharoopan's lips seeped through Gayathri's ears and savoured her entire body. She laughed as though she were being tickled.

Whenever she rocked with laughter, Satyakan usually felt intoxicated. But that day, for the first time, he experienced irritation.

"Stop it!" Satyakan commanded.

She muttered, as though possessed, "Will we exist at all, after death?"

Satyakan did not understand anything. He looked at the sky and into the Arya forest by turns, and murmured, "I'm in love with you. I have become so much a part of you that we cannot be separated. I love you!"

Hearing Satyakan's chant, Gayathri stopped walking. She listened carefully to something and called Megharoopan to her side. Then, returning to her former inebriated state, she told both her lovers, "See! The river Arya is flowing rapidly. Let's go to the other bank and sit there."

NINETEEN

Gayathri sat down, drunk with joy, between the daydreaming Megharoopan and the silent Satyakan. She had been observing them alternately for a long time. Realising that each was in his own private world, she stroked their arms, kissed each gently, and placed them on her thighs. Then, caressing their arms softly and pressing them against her breasts, she continued her love games.

But both men were totally oblivious of her overtures. Gayathri became incensed. The men pretended not to see it. Finally, extending the long fingers of her left hand, she touched Megharoopan's shoulder. She ran her fingers down his back, then rubbed his chest and went further and further down, spreading electric tendrils all over him. Her right hand stretched towards Satyakan and stroked him in a similar fashion. When both men came out of their thoughts, and were aroused, she made them lie down near the bank of the river, lay between them, and passionately muttered into their ears, "One... We are one!"

Megharoopan, who had always lost himself in such words until then, suddenly rose to his feet. Like a guilty child, he reminded Gayathri, "We have only this night ahead of us. We should decide what to do with it!"

She seemed not hear him.

Megharoopan spoke again, "Gayathri, this is a crucial night. We should decide what to do with it. Get up!"

She pleaded with Megharoopan, "That can wait, Megharoopa! Look! My left side is throbbing for you. Receive it. Even though Satyakan and I have been together since last night, he has enjoyed only the right side of me, over which he has rightful claim. Since then, look! And even now, my left side is eager to have you. Megharoopa, my dear Megharoopa, receive it!"

Even as she complained, amidst the explosion of suppressed lust, Megharoopan kept on muttering in despair, "Gayathri, my dear Gayathri! Let's think of something. Let's take a decision." Meanwhile Satyakan was indifferently shaking his feet near the riverbank.

Bursting into tears, Gayathri said, "I'm devastated."

Hearing that, Megharoopan cast aside all his thoughts, and pressed her left side to his body.

While melting into Megharoopan, Gayathri stretched her right arm, embraced Satyakan, and surrendered her right side to him. He savoured her lovingly.

Thus, surrendering her entire body to the two lovers, Gayathri felt deliciously empty and mumbled, "I live in you!"

TWENTY

Like a tree trunk covered over by a tracery of vines, Gayathri and Megharoopan slept in each other's arms in utter exhaustion near the riverbank. The little waves woke them up and teased them by recalling the love antics they had played the previous night. As the lovers began to stir, the mischievous wind, scooping up water from the river and drizzling drops on their nude bodies, murmured something. The infant sunrays pressed their greedy lips against Gayathri's breasts, that had been passionately sucked by Megharoopan and Satyakan, and reminded her about the passage of time.

That was when Megharoopan truly came to his senses. He called Satyakan and Gayathri, "Come, let's go to the garden. It's time for the guru's arrival!"

Gayathri walked into the river. The arms of the waves embraced her. Pushing aside the water that stuck out their tongues to lick her, as they usually did after her love games, Gayathri asked, "But we haven't thought about it at all! So, what do we do?"

Megharoopan replied, "There's nothing new for us to do. Everything will proceed according to what we had decided upon earlier."

Then, looking at Satyakan, he added, "Satyaka, my courage rests on your being with me!"

Getting up, Satyakan replied,

"I will be there. But if any single individual protests, I will support that person. I promise I won't oppose anything on my own!"

Gayathri did not utter a word.

Holding out his hand and pulling her out of the water, Megharoopan reminded her, "Come on! Let's go. It's time for the guru's arrival."

TWENTY-ONE

When Guru Arya appeared at the shore of the great sea of humans, Megharoopan stood right behind him. Next to him was an indifferent Gayathri, and following her, Satyakan who kept his anger in check. The guru turned to have a quick look. Seeing Megharoopan accompanied by Satyakan as well as a young lady who looked like a beautiful golden idol, he became intensely happy, and muttered to himself, "Everyone has surrendered themselves!"

Walking towards the shade of the absent Ashoka tree in the garden, Guru Arya looked at the people. He recognised that all of them looked similar, as they anxiously awaited their moment of liberation with a subservient attitude. There was no variety of emotions on display. All the humans had acquired the same expression.

On sighting Guru Arya, they called out confidently, "O guru! We are willing to sacrifice our lives as you instruct us so that we can be spared the sorrows and suffering on earth!"

When all the waves of that sea repeated it as a refrain in a cadence, the guru laughed. Seeing that, the people said once again, "O guru! How exactly should we give up our lives? Please instruct us on how to do it."

Guru Arya thought for some time.

They are searching for the very manner of self-sacrifice.

What servility! Their self- sacrifice should be conducted in the most glorious style.

Guru Arya's mind went over the Vedas and the epics. Eventually, he found the way out.

The most acclaimed one is to enter the holy fire. But there are various kinds of fire. Which is the most appropriate one for this occasion?

He turned to mythology. Finally, he came upon Swaha Devi, the consort of Agni Deva, the god of fire.

She embodies the elements of primeval Nature, symbolises radiance, and presides as the goddess of homes. In all these respects, she is the most appropriate choice. But the offspring she has by Agni Deva – Dakshinaagni, Garhapatnyaagni and Aahavaniyaagni – are undoubtedly superior. Ancient rules dictate that oblations offered during fire worship and other rituals have to be poured into a combination of various types of fire. Well, this too is a kind of fire ritual!

Therefore, Guru Arya concluded, the combination of all the three fires would be highly auspicious. He informed the people, "The glorious path to self-sacrifice is by entering the holy fire!"

The people unanimously agreed to it.

Guru Arya instructed them, "Each of you must come back with whatever substance is best suited for cremating yourself. We shall offer them together to a massive holy fire and sacrifice ourselves."

The people had only one face and, for that reason, only one voice. "Let that be so!"

The guru made a proclamation.

"This garden is the venue of our fire ritual. You must come back with *havis*, the offering for the holy fire."

As soon as they heard it, the people ran in different directions.

Guru Arya recalled that this would be the first massive self-sacrifice ever to take place in the universe. What he originally had in mind was a phased ritual. But the enthusiasm of the crowd inspired him to be really adventurous.

A joint fire – a mass self-sacrifice!

Guru Arya felt immensely gratified over his decision. He looked at Megharoopan. Megharoopan, heaving a huge sigh of relief, prostrated in front of the guru and prayed, "O guru! You showed us the path of deliverance, but we have nothing to offer you! Nothing except this, our physical bodies."

Lifting Megharoopan to his feet, the guru laughed uproariously.

Seeing an overwhelmed Megharoopan and hearing the dispassionate laughter of Guru Arya, Gayathri and Satyakan stood there, without blinking their eyes. They were dazed when they heard Megharoopan ask the guru:

"Why did you laugh, guru? I was merely revealing my heart!"

"Son, Megharoopa!" The guru spoke consolingly. "No-one is giving anyone anything. It is not possible for anyone to give anything to anyone. Everything is a sacrifice of the self."

Then, after meditating for a minute, Guru Arya spoke, as though imparting a secret, "You, your humans and your soil, all of you will be surrendering nothing but yourselves. Even the wind that blows here is full of its own self. It blows towards its own hot areas. You will understand all this by tomorrow, when you gain release from all forms of bondage on earth, when you get dissolved in ecstasy."

The guru's words made Megharoopan stand stock-still. It took him some time to come out of a state of self-forgetfulness. His eyes overflowed, his lips trembled, and an otherworldly glow glinted in his face. He said, "O guru! With your blessings, I'm already able to see the ultimate truth. I understand that what you utter is the eternal truth!"

He fell at Guru Arya's feet once again and offered his respects.

Lifting him, the guru said, "It's not time yet for the final decision, Megharoopan. You must wait out this night. You too must offer *havis* to the holy fire."

Then, looking at Gayathri and Satyakan, he enquired of Megharoopan, "You haven't introduced them to me!"

Apologising quickly, Megharoopan said, "Please forgive me, guru! I believe you've already recognised them. Do I really need to introduce them? I know about your special powers. But let me obey you. This is Satyakan, my soul mate. Or perhaps, you must see him as my alter ego. Better still, he is *me*! The same is true of Gayathri. She means everything to us. By her nature and her behaviour, she is mother in the morning, sister in the forenoon, goddess at noon, friend in the afternoon, lover in the evening and at dusk, and half our body at night!"

Gayathri touched Guru Arya's feet in reverence. He blessed her. Satyakan, on the other hand, stood there unmoving, offering a small, formal smile. The guru stared at him.

Satyakan, suspecting that the guru, long used to seeing only obsequious behaviour, might misconstrue his attitude as arrogance, said, "Guru, I don't have the habit of joining my palms or bowing my head to show respect. My backbone does not bend even a little. Megharoopan and Gayathri tell me that it is a disease. I console myself with the thought that I have become like this because of long years of carrying baskets of soil up the steep hill."

The guru laughed, and spoke in a prim tone, "No need for it, Satyaka. You need not bow before anyone. I understand your uniqueness from your very body language. But let me tell you something. Didn't you say that your backbone cannot bend itself? Be sure it does not break!"

Although everyone, Satyakan included, laughed at the guru's words, Satyakan felt slightly uneasy.

Does the guru's statement contain a mysterious message? If so, what does it portend?

But Satyakan could not follow his train of thought. The guru asked him,

"Satyaka, let me ask you something. And I'll be very frank with you. When I advised all the troubled residents of the saffron hill to accept *Mrityusutra* as an escape route, you were the only person who did not express any happiness over it. I observed it. I made note of it. What's your reason?"

Megharoopan and Gayathri were startled at the guru's question.

Could he have understood everything? Will Satyakan be the object of his ire? Will he alone be left out of the rescue act?

As the passing moments of apprehension whipped up a storm of uneasiness, Satyakan's voice sounded like a loud thunderclap, and rendered their worries irrelevant.

"O guru! I am desirous of the welfare of my humans. But equally, I'm upset at their sorrow. You need to understand only that much!"

The guru became silent. Megharoopan and Gayathri stood still. Only the dry breeze of the saffron hill kept blowing. Finally, coming out of his cocoon of silence, the guru spoke to Satyakan in a kind tone.

"Satyaka, right now my aim is to rescue the people of this place. I have come here to accomplish that. My duty is to show these suffering people a way out. Moreover, I have taken on the responsibility of leading them to the goal. And this is a truth that has emerged out of my own awareness. But if *anyone* opposes my efforts here, I'll have to give up everything."

On hearing the strong statements, Megharoopan looked at Satyakan pleadingly. Satyakan felt that Gayathri's face too wore a similar expression. She even appeared to be making a request. Eventually, not wanting to be an obstacle in anyone's path, Satyakan spoke candidly.

"O guru! Please don't misunderstand me. I'm only happy in the welfare of others. It pains me that I have to inform you I will feel sad at the destruction of the people. Don't let this ritual be cancelled, fearing my dissent. But should anyone in the saffron hill, of his or her volition, oppose this mass self-sacrifice, I will support that person to the hilt."

The guru became uneasy. Maybe that was why Gayathri intervened.

She said, "O guru! Like you, Satyakan is a *satyakaami*, a lover of truth. And he will remain so until the last breath of his life. You must trust him implicitly."

In order to impart courage to the guru, she continued, "Your instruction is acceptable to everyone here. No-one will oppose you."

The guru laughed and said to no-one in particular, "I understand Satyakan now, more than anyone else does. But that's the very cause of my uneasiness!"

Hearing this, Satyakan replied in a tone of total indifference, "O guru! We'll return with the *havis* as offering."

He called Megharoopan and Gayathri, "Come, Megharoopa. Come, Gayathri."

As they walked away, Guru Arya muttered to himself, "Let me prepare the fire altar."

TWENTY-TWO

While searching in the edge of the Arya forest for some object worthy of being offered as *havis*, Satyakan had a sudden insight.

What other object should I look for in order to cremate this body? Isn't the body itself enough?

He shared his idea with Megharoopan and Gayathri. They did not understand his point. Finally, he asked them, "Am I not capable of cremating myself? Aren't the material aspects of my body enough to cremate me?"

Gayathri saw it as a new revelation. She clung to his right side, kissed his ear, and whispered, "Satyaka, what you say is so true!" Then she muttered to herself, "When everything is available within, why go looking for it outside?" Her soliloquy became slightly louder. "In our urge to look outside for anything and everything all the time, we make fools of ourselves."

Megharoopan also felt that Gayathri's argument made perfect sense.

Everything resides in me. My body is enough to cremate me. The material aspects of my body!

Imbibing the essence of Satyakan's philosophy, Megharoopan said with a full heart, "My dear Satyaka, how right you are! Let's share this with our humans who are looking for *havis* to offer the holy fire."

But Gayathri stopped him.

"No! Let them find out for themselves what is best suited for their own cremation." Megharoopan could not oppose Gayathri. He merely kept on gazing at her.

Suddenly Gayathri became still, as though she had discovered something. Then, joyfully inhaling an otherworldly fragrance that had wafted from somewhere, she told her lovers, "Do you feel a musky breeze blowing? It's seducing me into a trance! Dear ones, this is our last night at the saffron hill. Let's make this night memorable!"

Then, looking upwards, she continued, "Look! The sky is studded with starflowers. Megharoopa, Satyaka! Let's shake the sky, and when the starflowers fall, let's wear them."

Not waiting for her lovers' responses, Gayathri, like a sleepwalker, called Megharoopan by name and lisped, "Aren't you Megharoopan, a friend of the clouds? Isn't the sky-tree within your reach? Haven't you told me that stars are flowers which bloom on the sky-tree, standing on the hill where clouds graze? Can't you see them? The sky-tree is heaving with flowers! Starflowers are blooming all over! Won't you stretch your arm above the clouds, pluck the starflowers, and deck my tresses with them?"

Then, calling Satyakan by name, she coaxed him lovingly, "My dear Satyaka! Is there anything you can't accomplish? Don't you see the moonbeam-petals falling? Pick them up and drizzle them over my body. But first, let me peel off my clothes! Won't you drape me with moonbeam-petals?"

Her voice became inebriated. "Megharoopa, Satyaka! Do you see the mattress on the skywalk? Let's lie down there!"

Unable to speak any further, she looked keenly and with intense longing at her lovers. Seeing no change in their attitude, she pleaded again, "Make me empty! Take your share of my mind and my body!"

Gayathri's sensual demands aroused Satyakan. He caught hold of her right arm, covered it with kisses, and sucked her right earlobe and eye. As she moaned fervently, he caressed her right breast and greedily licked the drops of ambrosia that trickled out.

Satyakan went into raptures. He dragged his lips downwards, ran his tongue over the right side of her tender stomach, just below her right breast, and rested his slack lips and tongue on the right bank of the deep navel, the whirlpool of passion. Going further down, his lips and tongue sought to slake an ancient thirst. Finally, the seeker of truth had a vision of the ultimate reality. He kissed her right knee, and searched for cool poise in her right ankle, the nerve centre of universal winter. Then, touching her right foot with his face, he prayed.

"Gayathri! O destroyer of suffering through the aeons! O goddess! Shackle me forever to these ineffable moments of joy, this pinnacle of ecstasy! I don't want freedom, O goddess! Make me your slave. Chain me here, to this foot of yours!"

All the while, Gayathri had been rocking gently on the waves of an unknown sensory euphoria. But still, a feeling of incompleteness suffocated her.

While drowning in the depths of uneasiness, she realised with disappointment that it was the sheer weight of her own left side that was weakening her.

Only her right side, savoured by its rightful owner, Satyakan, had become liberated. The left side of both her body and her mind was completely racked with thirst. Gayathri looked lustfully at Megharoopan.

By then, Megharoopan, unconscious of everything, was conversing with the infinite. Inserting her brimming left breast between Megharoopan's lips, she waited.

"My dear one!" she murmured. "Take in this ambrosia. Set me free!"

Megharoopan spat out her breast, and spoke helplessly, "I can't, Gayathri. I can't!"

She complained again. "Megharoopa, don't test me. The entire left side of my body is thirsting to have you. I can't help it. Receive what is due to you and liberate me!"

Caught in a moral dilemma, Megharoopan said, "Even if I set my mind to it, I can't, Gayathri. My mind is disturbed."

Gayathri wept again and attempted to inject frenzied lust into Megharoopan. But none of her efforts bore fruit.

Eventually, still caught in a dream-state, Megharoopan stated, "Gayathri, no worldly object, not even you, will be able to attract me hereafter. I understand death through *Mrityusutra*. I see death before me. I smell death. I touch death."

Buffeted by lust, heat and rage, Gayathri lamented to the infinite. Then she attempted to control herself. But everything was in vain. In the end, forgetting all sense of truth and moral decorum, abandoning all pious rituals, she tried to embrace Satyakan. She was prepared to give her left side also to Satyakan.

Satyakan, lying in a state of stupor, woke up with a start.

"No, Gayathri. I don't want anything that is forbidden. Especially your left side."

Gayathri wept. "Don't be cruel to me, Satyaka. Don't suffocate me!"

But Satyakan stopped her. "I will not receive anything that is not rightfully mine. Your left side is not mine. I don't want anything that is not mine."

When she compelled him again, Satyakan said categorically, "No, I'm a *satyakaami*, and I will remain a lover of truth until the end of my days. I will not take anything that is not mine."

Gayathri was shattered. All the suppressed lust within her burst forth. And the Arya forest, which had been lying sleeplessly, observed it silently.

TWENTY-THREE

The fire altar stood right in the middle of the garden. As tongues of fire leapt up from it, Guru Arya stood near it, as radiant as another flame. He observed the approaching lines of people with curiosity. The first to arrive was Gayathri.

Walking with outstretched arms, her breasts firm, eyes brimming with tears, and lips quivering, she had brought herself as *havis* to be offered to the holy fire.

Guru Arya looked at her with interest. She was not the golden idol-like, cheery-faced woman of yesterday. Rather, she appeared to be the symbol of bursting sorrow, caught in the depths of uneasiness and dissatisfaction.

What could be the reason for this change?

Although Guru Arya began to think about it, he forgot everything on seeing Satyakan coming just behind her.

Satyakan's eyes were sparkling with unusual courage. The glow of a firm decision had imparted a sheen to his face. He stretched out his arms reverentially, keeping them just below his broad chest, and surrendered himself as *havis* to the holy fire.

Behind him was Megharoopan who wore an indifferent expression. His movements were like those of a sleepwalker. He too brought himself as a *havis*.

The guru wanted to ask something to Gayathri, Satyakan

and Megharoopan on seeing them arrive as a singular *havis*-object. But he was completely taken aback when he observed that the surging crowds too were bringing themselves as an offering to the altar.

The guru was at once wonderstruck and confused. The residents of the saffron hill seemed to have only one face as they approached with one mind, intent on doing one deed, and came as one entity to jointly participate in the ritual! Through them, he saw that truth also had only one face.

Everyone is the same in front of death, everyone is equal!

As the master of the ceremony, when Guru Arya thought about the *havis*, he was overpowered by amazement.

Even the preceptor who is to lead the ritual is only one among equals!

Looking at the garden that was virtually spilling over with humans, Guru Arya directed them to stand in a circle around the fire altar. When they did as instructed, the guru lit the holy fire.

As the flames rose into the sky, the guru stared at them with unblinking eyes, in a trance, meditating on the flaming sun as well as the earth that held fire within her soul.

Guru Arya realised that only fire could outmatch the sun, and he conveyed this to the earth secretly. Although the earth had sought to escape the solar heat, the sun had pursued her relentlessly, caught her, and chained her to an orbit so that she would always pay obeisance at his fiery feet.

"Did you wish to see him defeated at any stage?" Guru Arya asked the earth. But he did not get even a small response. Undeterred, the guru uttered a mantra comparing the status of the sun and the fire.

"The human mind can conceive of only forms or idols. It is incapable of either internalising or imagining universal powers, including the omnipresent, invisible and imagined concept of God. It is not capable of containing these powers within specific and definite shapes either. That is why elements of the universe, like fire and the sun, became idols far back in time. Among them, the earliest was Agni or the god of fire. And the very same fire is burning brilliantly here now, rendering the sun dull in comparison."

Despite hearing this, there was no visible change in the earth's visage. The guru turned to his duties.

The fires have now engulfed the entire garden.

The guru stood looking at it for some time. He felt the fires shone more magnificently than the sun.

In a matter of minutes, all the humans on the earth will sacrifice themselves by appeasing the raging fire! Later, alone amidst the burnt-out fire pits, the earth will regret having shown cruelty to humans, and weep bitter tears. The sun, on the other hand, will be outshone by the incinerating and all-consuming power of fire!

Guru Arya looked at the earth which continued to revolve. Her eyes, filled with rage and heat, were closed. For a moment, Guru Arya even suspected that, suppressing all her screams deep within her soul, the earth was enjoying the sweet moments of revenge. Suddenly he asked the earth, "O Vasundhara, who ran away in fear of solar fire! Now, you have been made to carry real fire in your womb. I am going to save all the humans you cursed, with the help of the same fire that has been started on your surface. I am going to honour my promise. Now my pilgrimage is about to come to an end."

The guru looked at the earth once again. Suddenly, taking pity on the earth, who was quivering and whimpering under the weight of repressed anger, he began to console her.

"O Vasundhara! Don't weep! Ask the sun to liberate you."

Even at this point, Guru Arya was not sure whether the earth was distraught. Fearing that he would go into a sorrowful mood himself if he continued to look on for a long time, the guru spoke to the people of the saffron hill, "It's time to enter the holy fire. I shall be the first one to do it. The rest of you follow me!"

But the crowds protested.

"No! First, *we* will enter the holy fire. You should be the last."

Satyakan sought the guru's permission. "Please allow me to enter the holy fire!" he exclaimed.

But Megharoopan deterred him. "That shouldn't happen. If anyone withdraws sometime in between or at the very end of the ritual, you must be there for them. So, you should be the last."

Then Megharoopan appealed to the guru. He pleaded, "O guru! Grant me permission to enter the holy fire!"

But on hearing this, Gayathri stepped in to stop him.

"Megharoopan should enter the fire along with the guru," she said. "Isn't it inappropriate that the very person who took the lead in everything escapes first?"

Paying heed to her words, Megharoopan withdrew himself.

Gayathri now spoke to the guru: "O guru! Grant me permission to enter the holy fire!" Then she muttered to herself, "I'm dissatisfied, imperfect and need to hide myself somewhere!"

Nobody blocked her. The guru gave her his consent.

As instructed by the guru, Gayathri stepped back seven feet and then made a leap into the flames.

TWENTY-FOUR

All the humans of the saffron hill peered into the flames. They were expecting to see Gayathri's entry into the holy fire. But she did not fall into it.

What kind of magic is this?!

As they stood dumbfounded, the humans of the saffron hill saw a spectacle above the flames. Two strong arms stretched out, wrapped themselves around Gayathri, and held her aloft. Then, holding her close to the left side of his body, the owner of the arms walked slowly towards the humans of the saffron hill.

Along with him, an irate wind and the smell of burnt forest came blasting towards the saffron hill.

However, the wind became still in front of the flames. The fragrance that accompanied it began to dissolve into the breath exhaled by the crowd.

Enraged by the interruption caused to the escape ritual, Megharoopan, Satyakan, all the other people of the saffron hill and Guru Arya became disturbed. The people became restive. They surged forward. But Megharoopan stopped them.

Paying no attention to anything, a huge man, holding Gayathri close to his left side and cradling her against his chest, smiled slyly at the crowd. He waited, but seeing no response, lay Gayathri on the ground, looked at the crowd, and smiled again.

The people became further enraged.

This is a strange man who has never been seen at the saffron hill until now! Who could he be?

Satyakan had his suspicions.

Doesn't this man resemble the invisible form that occasionally flitted across my conscious mind, placing bans that caused suffocation within?

His suspicions grew.

Isn't he that same invisible man who was angry over the halting of the digging of wells and the scooping of soil for increasing the height of the hill? Isn't he the man who predicted dire consequences?

TWENTY-FIVE

The eyes of the unusually tall man had the colour of turquoise. His long, curly locks reaching up to the shoulders shook with every movement he made. The saffron hill residents felt that the man was definitely unique. His chest was broad, hands long, waist narrow, and calf muscles very firm.

Who is he? What's his intention?

They were full of doubts. Forgetting all about the hour of freedom, they stared at him.

After paying close attention to Gayathri lying unconscious on the ground and the raging flames, he observed Megharoopan and Satyakan. Then he looked at the crowd. He did not glance in the direction of Guru Arya at all.

Then at the most unexpected moment, making strange gestures, he looked at the residents of the saffron hill, and shouted, "O people..."

They did not respond. Until then, they had only been addressed as 'my humans'.

Looking at the anxious-looking people, the man said loudly, "I saw flames rising from the saffron hill. And billowing black clouds as well. Fearing that you might have fallen into a dangerous situation, I came here to rescue you. I'm Atmanathan."

There was a sudden movement in the crowd. Had they muttered Atmanathan's name? Or, expressed impatience over delay in their deliverance? The reason for their restlessness was not clear.

"I'm the invisible protector of the saffron hill!"

When he said that aloud, the people were startled. Megharoopan and Satyakan continued to stare at him. The man's appearance there was a mystery.

Not paying any attention to them, the man continued, "I had always been satisfied with your rituals, and when they got interrupted these last two days, I forgave you. And now, when I saw these flames, I was convinced you were in danger."

The crowd cowered in fear.

All the rituals had been performed at the saffron hill this far in the name of a belief. But now, it has become clear that those were expected to be done, and were based on truth!

As the people stood frightened, they had to face a barrage of question-arrows shot from Atmanathan's quiver.

"Why this fire pit? Why did you plan to cremate all your material aspects? What purpose will it serve? What were you hoping to achieve?"

In reply to the queries that came rapidly towards them, the crowd spoke in one voice, "We are about to enter the holy fire!"

"Why?"

Atmanathan's question carried a tone of authority. The crowd explained.

"This is the only path that will lead us away from our sorrows, suffering and troubles. Moreover, on entering the holy fire, we'll enjoy *Paramananda*."

What they heard in response was a scornful bellow of laughter. They could not see Atmanathan when he laughed. The raucous sound of hilarity was deafening. The echoes multiplied for a long time until they stopped all of a sudden. It felt as though the sound of thunderclaps and storm had just subsided. The next question from Atmanathan came unexpectedly.

"Who told you that if you give up your lives, your troubles will come to an end, and that you will attain *Paramananda*?"

Everyone spoke in a single voice. "Guru."

"Which guru?"

The people pointed him out.

"The person standing there. Guru Arya. Our saviour!"

Although the people, including Megharoopan, said that, Atmanathan did not look at Guru Arya at all. Rather, what he did was to sprinkle a few drops of water on Gayathri's face and revive her from unconsciousness.

She woke up suddenly. Her first response was as though she was trapped in an unfamiliar place. Then, gradually her demeanour changed.

Pressing her left side against the strong arms of Atmanathan, she asked anxiously, "Have I reached? Have I?"

"No!" Atmanathan's voice was thick. "You have not set out from any place. How then can you reach somewhere?"

"But what about my entry into the holy fire?"

In reply, what Atmanathan did was to shoot a counter-question, with the pride of authority.

"What right do you have to cremate and destroy this body that God created, and Time as well as Nature nourished?"

Gayathri was confused. She stood hesitant, like a guilty child. Yet she felt bliss inside.

I'm enclosed within a pair of strong arms. I feel very secure and satisfied!

But repressing all that, she merely glanced at Atmanathan, as though she was just coming out of light sleep.

Sensing an attitude of complete surrender in that look, Atmanathan drew her close to him, and asked the people, "Imagine that a person, who has been punished for grave mistakes and sentenced to imprisonment at the saffron hill, escapes. What will you do?"

Hearing that unexpected and irrelevant question, the people stood dumbfounded. Megharoopan, however, understood the hidden intent of the question. Satyakan flew into a rage, and Guru Arya began to laugh.

Disregarding all of them, Gayathri pressed her left side

greedily towards Atmanathan. She forgot herself in the wave of exhilaration that swept over her. "Tell me!" she cried.

Atmanathan urged the people, "How will you treat a person who breaks jail?"

"Catch hold of him." The people replied unanimously.

"And then?"

"Put him back in prison, with an additional penal term for breaking jail."

The people thus conveyed the rules that prevailed at the saffron hill.

Atmanathan's face lit up. Adopting a condescending tone, he said, "In that case, I've saved you from a major crime, and from the punishment it would have brought upon your heads."

The people looked at one another impatiently. Sensing their uneasiness, Megharoopan turned to Guru Arya for a reply. A scornful smile was just beginning to sprout on the guru's face.

Satyakan found it hard to control his anger.

Eventually, Megharoopan himself asked Atmanathan, "What are you talking about? We don't understand anything."

Atmanathan's reply came quickly.

"You are prisoners of the saffron hill. Your attempt at self-sacrifice is tantamount to breaking jail!"

Megharoopan still did not understand anything. The people also became irritated. So, Megharoopan asked Atmanathan again, "Please speak more clearly. Why do you delay our time of liberation?"

In reply, Atmanathan looked into the infinite. Then, as if in a dream, he said, "You, who took birth in the saffron hill, are prisoners. The various crimes you committed, knowingly or otherwise, in your previous birth, attracted this punishment, this birth in the saffron hill."

After stopping for a while to assess the people's response, Atmanathan continued, "The terms and the methods of punishment are decided by the degree of seriousness of your mistakes and crimes. This is divine justice. The punishments are regulated according to it, and Nature executes them. In that way, all of you have become prisoners."

Having said this much, Atmanathan remained silent for some time. What he said next had a strange sonority about it: "Each one has a separate term of punishment. It may be sixty years for one person, eighty for another, twenty for yet another. That constitutes your lifetime here. That's also your prison term. That's how long you'll be incarcerated."

Slyly observing the silence that descended on the people when they heard all that, Atmanathan continued, "Haven't you seen a few instances of infant death? We say that those children passed on. But that's because they had been sentenced to only two or three years in prison. And that maybe either rigorous or simple imprisonment. A few may lead a very tough life with serious mental and physical problems. That's rigorous imprisonment. You might also have seen people flow along smoothly, untouched even by the heaviest of sorrows. That's simple imprisonment. All said and done, this prison term, whatever the duration, has to be endured."

After a few moments of silence, when Atmanathan spoke, the very rhythm of his statements changed. "The prison term has to be served completely. As for natural death – that signals release after the completion of the term. That is, once you have suffered the punishment fully, remaining in jail throughout the stipulated time, death will come calling. And those who complete their prison term and die, will be dissolved in the divine elements and granted bliss. That is the real *Paramananda*."

What he uttered next were words dripping with sarcasm. "But the ritual that you have set out to conduct – this self-sacrifice by entering the fire – is against Nature. This is a jail break before you've served your term. And the punishment meted out for the crime is another birth and life of hellish torture. That'll be the term of imprisonment."

Then he continued in absolute seriousness. "Maybe this attempt of yours is because you never received a vision of the truth. Now that you know what the truth is, why do you want to slide into mistakes? Do you still imagine you'll be able to escape by doing these foolish acts? What will you be able to do by hoodwinking or defying God? So, return to your rituals without provoking the ire of the Almighty!"

By now, his statements had taken on the complexion of a threat. Possibly because of that, by the time he reached the end of his speech, Gayathri pressed her left side hard against him and collapsed at his feet.

"Natha... Atmanathan... Lord of the soul! Please save us!"

As soon as Megharoopan, who had been standing still all the while, saw the change in Gayathri, he kneeled in front of Atmanathan.

"Natha... Atmanathan! What you say is the ultimate truth. What a grave sin you've rescued us from!"

On hearing that, all the people followed in Megharoopan's footsteps, and kneeled in front of Atmanathan.

Satyakan, unable to contain his anger, closed his eyes. Inwardly, he wailed: *What a betrayal this is!*

Seeing, hearing and experiencing everything, Atmanathan smiled a mysterious smile, quite like a victor, while observing someone in the far distance. Or, was this all a show, meant for someone to see?

The angry wind, that had come along with Atmanathan towards the fire altar at the saffron hill, now cast off its inertia, and began to blow hard in all directions. The pungent smell of the dry forest that had accompanied the wind, dissolved completely in the breath of the people of the saffron hill, and spread in all four directions.

TWENTY-SIX

Satyakan's mind was conflict-ridden.

How quickly have the humans of the saffron hill switched loyalties! Megharoopan's change of stand is simply unbelievable! And Gayathri? She, who used to revel in diving headlong into unseen depths of lust, has shown a fickleness that is disgusting! Megharoopan had received his vision of truth from Guru Arya. And now he's genuflecting in front of Atmanathan! What is to be done?

Satyakan observed Guru Arya. The guru appeared unfazed. With mounting curiosity, he watched the people who had earlier displayed servility and were now exuding hostility. Then he looked at Megharoopan and Gayathri with pity. Eventually, gazing at Satyakan, and seeming to take a decision, the guru slowly walked towards Atmanathan.

The convergence of two suns! Satyakan told himself.

TWENTY-SEVEN

Guru Arya approached Atmanathan and greeted him. But Atmanathan was not only reluctant to reciprocate the courtesy but also insistent that the conversation between them be conducted in private.

Agreeing to Atmanathan's condition, Guru Arya asked him, "Why are you cheating the people like this? Let them escape!"

Atmanathan gave his reply in a low, secretive whisper that reeked of absolute scorn.

"They do not have the permission to escape. If they escape, what will happen to this place? What will happen to us? Who will undertake all these activities?"

Then, after pausing for a moment, he continued in the same tenor, "I am entrusted with the responsibility of preventing their escape and of shackling them here. I have no hesitation in claiming that I am doing it brilliantly. I will accomplish it whatever obstacles come my way! And I will use whatever means it takes to finish my task."

What followed was an explanation.

"Making them dig wells where there's no water and instructing them to carry the clayey soil up the hill are all part of it. All those instructions about increasing the height of the hill by piling up soil, about making the summit touch the sky, and about building a path to heaven are meant to give them hope. You see, if people are made to undertake heavy labour in pursuit of a goal that cannot ever be achieved, their attention will not waver. They will concentrate exclusively on the task at hand without focusing on anything else, without interfering in any other business. And here, an effort was made to destabilise that principle."

Atmanathan's rage did not subside. It came surging forth in the form of harsh words.

"Do you know how much I had to struggle to overcome the crisis you precipitated? Did you notice that, as the last resort, I had to read the people's minds and talk about sins of the previous births, divine wrath and imprisonment and so on? Sin and God are the most powerful intoxicants. And didn't the people fall for it!"

As Atmanathan continued his victory speech, Guru Arya was observing him keenly and evaluating him. Atmanathan was standing right in the middle of the crowd, revealing the stratagems he had employed to exploit them! What an irony!

It filled Guru Arya with anxiety when he realised the sad truth that Atmanathan was arrogantly describing the ruses he was employing to abuse a whole community of followers, either for the sake of fulfilling the malicious desires or evil designs of some unknown persons or for serving the selfish interests of some individual or individuals.

Atmanathan had absolutely no qualms about admitting that the back-breaking work of the people of the saffron hill – to dig perpetually dry wells and continuously carry soil to the top of the hill – were all vain efforts. It seemed there were saffron hills spread across all the continents of the earth. And in each of them, digging of wells and carrying of soil were going on relentlessly. What Atmanathan's handlers wanted was that the people who were put on these tasks should not focus on anything else, do anything else, or go anywhere else. Atmanathan did not have any inhibitions about confessing that those who made people work and issued commands would always remain invisible.

Without any sense of shame, Atmanathan also said that servility was as intoxicating as obedience. It was this intoxicant that had put all the saffron hills of the earth in a state of stupor. There was no mantra more potent than this stupefaction to exploit human resources to the maximum! And no strategy more effective!

Atmanathan was very eager to allege that Guru Arya had arrived with his *Mrityusutra* in order to torpedo this entrenched belief. His charge was that Guru Arya and his *Mrityusutra* were the adversary's weapons aimed at destroying the monopoly of power over the saffron hill and the hard labour done there. Since that attempt had been foiled, Guru Arya was expected to leave without uttering a word. Otherwise, he would have to face consequences.

Guru Arya realised that Atmanathan had asked for a private audience with him amidst the thronging people primarily to convey this point. But he did not succumb to any threat.

TWENTY-EIGHT

On seeing that Guru Arya was firm in his defiance, Atmanathan spoke to the crowd.

"Your guru is abetting your jail break!" he said. Then he made his demand: "Please give him a fitting reply!"

Hearing that, Megharoopan appeared to be ready for anything. Taking on an attitude of aggression, he stared at the guru and hollered, "Betrayer! You forced us to commit a mistake!"

In response, Satyakan pounced, staring as if he would burn Megharoopan to a cinder. But the guru remained unruffled. He stopped Satyakan.

"Don't, son! Megharoopan *has* to speak like this! He cannot but speak in this manner!" Then, after stopping for a moment, he remarked, "I need to know what the people have to say."

Megharoopan became angry once again, exclaiming, "My humans share my stand on the issue! You betrayer! But my humans will not be cheated again!"

Guru Arya looked at the crowd. He suddenly noticed that their faces resembled Megharoopan's. They began to attack him with extreme aggression.

"Betrayer! Betrayer! Betrayer!"

Guru Arya felt utterly devastated. As he began to fall backwards, Satyakan held him. Leaning against Satyakan's knees, the guru stared at the flames raging in the fire altar.

TWENTY-NINE

The crowd, driven by irrepressible rage, was straining at the leash. Atmanathan, with one arm wrapped around Gayathri's left side and the other thrown over Megharoopan, walked exultantly towards the middle of the garden. The crowd waited eagerly for his command.

"We cannot let this sanyasi get away. He must suffer the punishment for attempting to betray us. We should imprison him. Let's chain him, as we do a mad dog!"

As soon as they heard these words from Atmanathan, the crowd surged towards Guru Arya. Megharoopan led the people. Gayathri, oblivious of everything happening around her, clung to Atmanathan's left shoulder.

As the people came charging in full throttle, Satyakan stepped in their way. He was like a mountain that could block any storm cloud and make it rain. The people stopped.

Satyakan shouted, "I will destroy everything! And I can do it on my own! Don't you dare go near him! Don't you dare touch the guru!"

Megharoopan was the first one to defy that warning and step forward. The crowd followed him. But Atmanathan doubted whether Megharoopan or the people could defeat Satyakan.

If anything goes wrong now, everything will come crashing down!

Even as Atmanathan was about to open his bag of tricks, Guru Arya intervened. Having grasped the gravity of the conflict, he stopped Satyakan with a firm hand.

"Satyaka, move aside. Let them do what they want."

Satyakan fumed. "No! That can't happen. I will not allow it. I will not stand a mute spectator when you, who came alone to rescue us, are attacked!"

Observing Satyakan's words and the crowd's reaction, Atmanathan tried to pour oil over troubled waters.

"They won't do anything, Satyaka. They'll bind him as a symbolic gesture of their revenge. That's all."

Satyakan's blood boiled.

Suddenly Guru Arya stood and spoke to Satyakan in a soft but commanding manner. "Step behind me, Satyaka. Let them tie me up. That serves my need too!"

Satyakan had no alternative. But he said to the people, "If you do anything other than bind the guru, if even a speck of dust were to fall on his body, none of you will remain alive. And neither will the saffron hill! Nor even Atmanathan!"

The residents of the saffron hill were sure that this was not a mere threat. It was an inviolable decision made by Satyakan, the lover of truth.

Then, cursing himself, wailing, and drowning in his moral quandary, Satyakan stepped back and closed his eyes. "I don't want to see anything, hear anything or know about anything!"

The seething crowd surrounded Guru Arya from all sides.

THIRTY

When he opened his eyes, Satyakan saw Guru Arya bound by millions and millions of ropes. Yet his face looked serene. Satyakan could hardly control himself.

What ingratitude this is!

As Satyakan stood confused, caught in a moral dilemma, the words of the people and Atmanathan fell on his ears simultaneously.

"Satyaka! For the time being, we have forgiven your anger!"

The words stopped for a moment. Then the flow continued.

"All the humans of the saffron hill have tied up this fake God-man. But his body has some space left, for one more rope to be tied by a man. And that man is you. Here's the rope. Tie up this con man who tried to orphan your saffron hill. Let your stamp of rejection too be fixed on him."

When all the shouts subsided, Satyakan tried to find the source of all this noise. All the humans of the saffron hill, Megharoopan and Gayathri, all of them were hollering, along with Atmanathan.

Satyakan could not tolerate it anymore. Using words that came from the depths of his soul, he said in no uncertain terms, "No! I will not tie up this righteous man, this saviour. The signs of my ingratitude will not be stamped on him!"

Atmanathan, quick to anger, immediately said something to provoke the people. And it had the intended effect. Even Megharoopan's face went livid with rage. Seeing this, Atmanathan not only had second thoughts but was also stricken with anxiety.

What if the reaction of the people backfires?

All the while, Gayathri remained immersed in Atmanathan.

Atmanathan told himself that he should not have any prejudgement against the reaction of the people. He slyly approached Satyakan, and remarked, "This is not to punish him. This is only an attempt to establish that, whatever be the circumstances, the people of the saffron hill are a single entity. With that in mind, Satyaka, you too must bind the guru."

Although Satyakan wished to protest again, a voice within convinced him that he could use this act of compromise as a weapon. Immediately he presented it as a practical instruction.

"Aren't we tying up the guru in the name of a belief... so that he doesn't run away? Let's not do it. I shall stand guard over him. I shall be his watchman for the people of the saffron hill. I shall ensure the guru doesn't escape."

The people agreed to it raucously. Satyakan's suggestion was acceptable. But Atmanathan felt he was trapped in a predicament. When he was about to say something about it, Gayathri spoke on behalf of the residents of the saffron hill.

"There's no need for any fear. Satyakan is a *satyakaami*, a lover of truth. He will not violate it under any circumstance. You may believe Satyakan absolutely."

Megharoopan endorsed it, confirming, "Yes, he is a *satyakaami*. We believe him."

The people agreed to it. They said, "We have faith in Satyakan. Let him stand guard."

Atmanathan could not say anything in protest. Stroking Gayathri, who was seeping into him, and repressing all the anger that was welling up in him, he announced, "Let this fake God-man lie here as our prisoner. Let Satyakan stand guard. Let the universe know that this is our revenge!"

Then, without waiting for any further response, Atmanathan told the people, "All of you may return. You may go back to your old rituals and tradition."

Even as he was sending the people back, his mind was busy plotting new stratagems.

Satyakan stood there for a long time watching all the people, including Megharoopan and Gayathri, as they retreated.

THIRTY-ONE

Satyakan thought that Megharoopan would turn back to look at him at least once. But no! He did not.

Gayathri has changed beyond recognition. Mesmerised by Atmanathan's physical strength, she seems to be getting completely dissolved in him. Or, has she disappeared into him altogether?

Satyakan felt utterly crushed. He quivered and wept.

THIRTY-TWO

To Guru Arya, who lay bound, even self-torture was exhilarating. But there was one thing – the contempt shown by the earth was more than he could endure. And at one point, he could not but respond to it.

"O Vasundhara! You have succeeded in chaining the poor humans to yourself. Are you so afraid to be alone? Do you still want to see all these humans wallow in sorrow and misery? Poor humans!"

But Guru Arya's words did not have even the least impact on the earth. Rather, he saw the earth laughing heartily, concealing thousands and thousands of sarcastic meanings within.

THIRTY-THREE

Satyakan, who kept looking at all the ropes binding Guru
Arya, suddenly moved towards him. He conversed with the
guru without uttering any words. The guru, realising that
Satyakan had arrived at some decision, tried to stop him by
moving his eyes. But Satyakan, summoning all the logical
arguments that came to his mind, appealed to the guru.

"O guru! I seek your pardon on behalf of the saffron hill.
You must understand that this is the first time I have bowed
in front of anyone. Please forgive us."

Then, placing his hands on the knots, he asked, "May I
untie these knots and set you free?"

Suddenly fire spread across the guru's eyes. He stopped
Satyakan vehemently.

"Satyaka! You are the embodiment of truth and the moral
values you believe in. You should not destroy it for anyone.
Not even for me!"

Satyakan disagreed with him.

"No, guru. I'm going to free you. It's true that my truth and
moral values are more precious than myself. But they tell me
that I should release you."

The guru spoke forcefully.

"Don't, Satyaka! You promised your people that you

would stand guard over me. And they believed you. You must not betray their trust. You must not abandon truth."

Thus, Guru Arya continued to dissuade him.

"In that case, guru, I'm going to abandon my truth and my moral values, and release you. Of what worth am I if I can't do at least this much in expiation of the sin committed by the ingrate people of the saffron hill? What can I do?"

Saying so, he began to untie the knots, one by one. But Guru Arya did not allow it. Finally, when none of his logical arguments seemed to work with Satyakan, he played his trump card.

"Satyaka, you won't obey even me, isn't it so? Alright! You may untie the binds. But let me tell you something. Even if you release me, I won't leave this place. I will lie here itself. Moreover, I'll tell the people of the saffron hill that I tried to escape. Then, they'll start torturing me. Do you want to see that? If you do, release me. On the other hand, if you take me away forcibly, I'll gain notoriety for having attempted to flee. That'll be too hard for me to bear!"

The guru's words put Satyakan in a quandary. He flung his arms up in the air, and stood still for a long time, staring into the infinite.

In the middle of that long spell of silence, Satyakan had a flash of insight. He looked at the guru. The guru's face was calm, and a smile was spreading across his face. Like moonbeams dispelling darkness, it shone light on Satyakan. That stream of light seemed to have a voice. The voice of Guru Arya!

"Satyaka, you have overpowered me! Your love, sacrifice, commitment, your integrity, so evident in your not abandoning your people even in a critical situation and always being there for them, all these are overwhelming! If I were to keep any secret from you at this point of time, that would be a great sin!"

Saying so, Guru Arya looked into the infinite, went into a trance for a long time, and then spoke.

"Satyaka, everything was fake. All that you saw, heard and experienced, everything was false. Even I, myself!"

He went into silence once again. Then, as an aside, he muttered, "After a certain stage, no-one can keep a secret!"

Guru Arya spoke with candour.

"*Mrityusutra* was implemented here in order to find out how long the rite of liberation would last. It was a secret means to weed out excess humans. And after achieving that end, some ruse would have been brought up to stop it midway."

He continued to speak along the same lines. Finally, on seeing the face of truth, Satyaka became blind. On hearing the voice of truth, Satyakan became deaf. On absorbing the essence of truth, Satyakan became mute.

Bowing at the soles of the guru's feet, Satyakan asked in a silent tongue.

"What should we do next? Is there no way of escape for my humans, O guru?"

"No!"

The guru was predicting the future.

"As long as they remain unlike themselves!"

Then he quickly went on to complete the half-uttered statement.

"As long as I, and people like me, remain here, neither you nor your humans will find a way to escape."

Assimilating the essence of those words, Satyaka spoke in a tone audible only to himself.

"My soil... my humans!"

THIRTY-FOUR

Satyakan felt that his complaints were getting heard somewhere. He also perceived that the indifference of the sun and the helplessness of the earth were causing the fire of anger to burn in someone's eyes. He was convinced that someone was judging Guru Arya's failure and Atmanathan's victory. He realised that his own stand as well as Megharoopan and Gayathri were also being scrutinised very carefully. But it was not clear to him who was doing it or from where.

At first, Satyakan thought of enquiring about it with Guru Arya. Then he abandoned the idea altogether. It was true that the guru had revealed certain facts. But Satyakan wondered whether the guru was an accomplice in the whole scheme.

As he stood there confused, staring into the infinite, he had a revelation. An omnipresent, invisible presence was directing everything.

When his conviction grew stronger, despite not knowing who, what or where it was, Satyakan looked at the infinite and bowed in reverence.

Then suddenly, startling Satyakan himself, a riotous sequence of unique sounds seemed to take on a visible form and give a reply.

"I am a disembodied voice..."

As the sounds came down in a shower of words, Satyakan

tried to visualise their form. But crushing all his efforts, those words fell on his ears in an authoritative tone.

"Despite knowing that your efforts were utterly purposeless, Satyaka, why were you and your humans involved in all that difficult labour? If your aim was to wipe out sorrows and suffering, couldn't you have tried to understand them before doing that hard work?"

It stopped for a while and then continued in a stern manner.

"Sorrow is a reality. So is suffering. But sorrow does not strike without a reason. It has a definite cause. And that cause is desire. By opposing desire, you can do away with grief. Suffering is also self-created. If you avoid the factors that destroy health, you can control suffering too. Don't these constitute release from sorrows and suffering?

"You had these solutions. Yet what did you do? Is there any justification for your vain efforts? You believed that if the hill on the earth could be raised to the skies and if a bridge could be built through the skies, you could physically enter heaven. And in order to achieve that goal, you put yourselves through untold troubles. But were your beliefs rationally justifiable? Likewise, you kept on digging wells all over the valley. Was it for scooping out clayey soil or for drawing water? You were directed to keep digging the wells until you found water. But none of the wells yielded it. Yet why didn't you give it some thought? Were all your vain efforts made without realising that you would never hit water?"

Having said this much, the words took on a tone of empathetic softness.

"Those who put you on these fruitless tasks knew the truth. The truth that water could be found in plentiful quantities not in the valley, where you dug wells, but in the aquifers hidden at the top of the saffron hill. Wasn't the water drawn through those bore wells used to slake your thirst? All your pointless work was done in ignorance of this fact. If you had known it, would you have set out to dig wells, carry soil or sacrifice yourselves?"

What followed was advice that inspired obedience.

"Try to overcome death and attain immortality by acquiring knowledge. Only if you fail in that attempt need you surrender your life. Isn't that the truth?

"You made arrangements to set up a fire altar obeying instructions from someone you didn't know anything about! Then, when you heard selfish advice from another source, you got prepared to dig wells in barren ground and to carry soil. Aren't you ashamed of your activities?"

Then, the voice became harsh.

"Is there any justice in cheating the people of the saffron hill in this manner? Is there any justification for allowing yourselves to be cheated so?"

Satyakan realised that the criticism of the disembodied voice was heard not only by him but Guru Arya also who was standing near him, as well as Atmanathan, standing some distance away, and all the residents of the saffron hill.

As soon as the voice of the disembodied entity began to boom, a humid gust of wind mysteriously took birth from it and drove the words into the ears of each and every human of the saffron hill. The repercussions were immediate. All the residents of the saffron hill, led by Megharoopan, returned to the garden, and stood near Satyakan.

Though still bound, Guru Arya appeared tranquil and observed everything. But all the while, Gayathri remained unaware of the happenings around her. She was passionately yearning to enter Atmanathan.

THIRTY-FIVE

The residents of the saffron hill felt that the disembodied voice was clearing the right path for them. Their eyes, ears and consciousness longed to see that invisible power. Despite not getting a glimpse of it, those who imagined the location of the source point of the sound, focused their attention in that direction. Soon, their ears filled with the ambrosial sounds of the disembodied voice.

"O humans! Be yourselves. Belong to yourselves. Reduce the distance between you and your true self."

After a pause, the sound flowed again.

"Understand your soil. It is not meant to be raised. Rather, it should be used to sow seeds in and raise crops on. Plant your feet on the soil and stand firmly on it."

The people laughed excitedly on hearing the divine sounds. Megharoopan and Satyakan strained their ears in the direction of the voice. Gayathri, however, heard nothing. Driven by some impulse, she had now detached herself from Atmanathan and become eager to insert herself secretly between Megharoopan and Satyakan. By then, the divine sounds swept over them in the form of advice.

"Don't have any feelings of hostility towards the sun. It is the gravitational power of the sun that keeps all the planets and the satellites in the solar system in their assigned places.

Similarly, realise that the energy produced by the sun comes from the fusion of atoms at an extremely high temperature. And it is this solar energy that maintains life on the earth. Therefore, pay respects to the sun.

"Now, about the earth. Earth is your mother. Your all-suffering mother who forgives you even when you dig into her, and break her heart; who understands your needs, and voluntarily satisfies them.

"Also understand certain facts about your garden. No plant, not even a blade of grass, can grow on clayey soil. It is because of the clayey soil that no plant grows in your garden and no flower blooms. So, remove the clayey soil, prepare the ground, sow seeds, and plant saplings. Let flowers bloom for the sake of your children."

When there was a pause in the flow, Megharoopan and Satyakan chanted a mantra loudly.

"We, the humans of the saffron hill, bow to the owner of the voice that we hear!"

The people repeated it.

On hearing the phrase 'saffron hill' repeatedly, the harshness of the musical sound grew intense.

"Understand that this is not a saffron hill. This is the soil where your ancestors reaped gold. If you work together in harmony, you will be able to convert it to its former glory. The hill will yield gold. The hill of gold!"

The floodgates of happiness opened among the people. "We shall obey!"

They spoke in one voice, and the reply came immediately.

"What is required is not obedience but observance of a ritual. Not a blind ritual fuelled by obedience but a ritual done in a spirit of self-surrender. A soul ritual!"

The people agreed to it loudly. Then they repeated their demand, as though saying a prayer.

"Please grant us a direct vision of the owner of the voice that showed us the right path!"

The reply was quick.

"Don't you see that I am you? Or, to put it differently, you are me! Look into yourself and you will see me."

The people did not understand anything. They were highly confused.

Eventually, encouraged by Megharoopan and Satyakan, when they asked for an explanation, the reply left them speechless with wonderment.

"Don't I exist inside you? Isn't it true that only you can see your inner self? Therefore, try to discover your true self inside yourself. And there, I reside!"

When the essence of those words dawned on the people, a fragrance-bearing, light breeze that had never before blown across the saffron hill, wafted in from somewhere and caressed everyone. Gradually, the whole place became cool and aromatic. The people recognised that it was the breath exuding from themselves. And as they looked on, the body of the voice appeared clearly, riding the wings of that breeze. The sight filled them with amazement.

At this point of time, the sun brought down the heat considerably. Vasundhara, the earth, who had until then, tied up her hair in a knot bun, let it down casually, and the season-flowers – spring, autumn and winter – fell from her tresses.